Rebecca Sophia Clarke

Fairy book

.

Rebecca Sophia Clarke

Fairy book

ISBN/EAN: 9783337235000

Printed in Europe, USA, Canada, Australia, Japan

Cover: Foto ©Andreas Hilbeck / pixelio.de

More available books at **www.hansebooks.com**

CRISTOBAL. Page 32.

LITTLE PRUDY SERIES.

———◆———

FAIRY BOOK.

BY

SOPHIE MAY.

———◆———

BOSTON:

LEE AND SHEPARD,

(Successors to Phillips, Sampson, & Co.)

1865.

THIS

BOOK OF FAIRY TALES

IS DEDICATED

TO LITTLE BESSIE.

LITTLE PRUDY SERIES.

BY SOPHIE MAY.

———⸰⸰⟩⸰⟨⸰⸰———

CONTENTS.

FAIRY BOOK.

---∘∘⦂◆⦂∘∘---

INTRODUCTION.

WHILE Prudy was in Indiana visiting the Cliffords, and in the midst of her trials with mosquitoes, she said one day, —

"I wouldn't cry, Aunt 'Ria, only my heart's breaking. The very next person that ever dies, I wish they'd ask God to please stop sending these awful skeeters. I can't bear 'em any longer, now, certainly."

There was a look of utter despair on Prudy's disfigured face. Bitter tears were trickling from the two white puff-balls which had been her eyes; her forehead and cheeks were of a flaming pink, broken into little snow-drifts full of stings: she looked as if she had just been rescued from an angry bee-hive. Altogether, her appearance was exceedingly droll; yet Grace would not allow herself to smile at her afflicted little cousin. "Strange," said she, "what makes our mosquitoes so impolite to strangers! It's a downright shame, isn't it, ma, to have little Prudy so imposed upon? If I could only amuse her, and make her forget it!"

"Oh, mamma," Grace broke forth again suddenly, "I have an idea, a very brilliant idea! Please listen, and pay particular attention; for I shall speak *in a figure*, as Robin says. There's a certain small individual who is not to understand."

"I wouldn't risk that style of talking," said Mrs. Clifford, smiling; "or, if you do, your figures of speech must be *very* obscure, remember."

"Well, ma," continued Grace with a significant glance at Prudy, " what I was going to say is this: We wish to treat certain young relatives of ours very kindly ; don't we, now? — certain afflicted and abused young relatives, you know.

"Now, I've thought of an entertainment. Ahem ! Yesterday I entered a certain Englishman's house," — here Grace pointed through the window towards Mr. Sherwood's cottage, lest her mother should, by chance, lose her meaning, — " I entered a certain Englishman's house just as the family were sitting down to the table, — *festal board*. I mean.

" They were talking about mistle-toe boughs, and all sorts of old-country customs ; and then they said what a funny time they had one Christmas, with the youngest, about the *mizzle*, as he called it : do you remember, ma? do you understand ?"

"You mean little Harvey? Oh, yes."

"Pray do be careful, ma! Then Mr. Sherwood said to his — I mean, the *hat* said to the *bonnet*, that there were some wonderful — ahem — legends, about genii and sprites and — and so forth; not printed, but *written*, which the boy liked to hear when he was 'overgetting' the measles. A certain lady, not three inches from your chair, ma, was the one who wrote them; and now" —

Prudy had turned about, and the only remnants of her face which looked at all natural — that is, the irises and pupils of her swollen eyes — were shining with curiosity.

"There, now, what is it, Gracie? what is it you don't want me to hear?"

Grace laughed. "Oh, nothing much, dear: never mind."

"You oughtn't to say 'Never mind,'" pursued Prudy: "my mother tells me *always* to mind."

"I only mean it isn't any matter, Prudy."

"Oh! do you? Then don't you care for my skeeter-bites? You always say, 'Never mind!' I didn't know it wasn't *any matter.*"

"Now, ma," Grace went on, "I want to ask you where are those I-don't-know-what-to-call-'ems? And may I copy them, Cassy and I, into a book, for a certain afflicted relative?"

"Yes, yes, on gold-edged paper!" cried Prudy, springing up from the sofa; "oh, do, do; I'll love you dearly if you will! Fairy stories are just as nice! What little Harvey Sherwood likes, *I* like, and I've had the measles; *but* I shouldn't think his father and mother'd wear their hat and bonnet to the dinner-table!"

"Deary me!" laughed Grace; "how happened that little thing to mistrust what I meant?"

"It would be strange if a child of her age, of ordinary abilities, should *not* understand," remarked Mrs. Clifford, somewhat amused. "Next time you wish to ask me any thing confidentially, I advise you to choose a better opportunity."

"When may she, Aunt 'Ria?" cried Prudy, entirely forgetting her troubles; "when may she write it, Aunt 'Ria, she and Cassy?"

"A pretty piece of folly it would be, wouldn't it, dear, when you can't read a word of writing?"

"But Susy can a little, auntie; and mother can a great deal: and I'll never tease 'em, only nights when I go to bed, and days when I don't feel well. Please, Aunt 'Ria."

"Yes, ma, I know you can't refuse," said Grace.

Mrs. Clifford hesitated. "The stories are

yellow with age, Grace; they were written in my girlhood: and they are rather torn and disarranged, if I remember. Besides, my child, my flowing hand is difficult to read."

"Oh, mamma, I think you write beautifully! splendidly!"

"Another objection," continued Mrs. Clifford: "they are rather too old for Prudy, I should judge."

"But I keep a-growing, Aunt 'Ria! Don't you s'pose I know what fairy stories mean? They don't mean any thing! You didn't feel afraid I'd believe 'em, did you? I wouldn't believe 'em, I *promise* I wouldn't; just as true's I'm walking on this floor!"

"Indeed, I hope you would not, little Prudy; for I made them up as I went along. There are no fairies but those we have in our hearts. Our best thoughts are good fairies; and our worst thoughts are evil fairies."

"Oh, yes, auntie, I know! When we go bathing in the ocean, Susy says, 'Let's be all clean, so the spirit of the water can enter our hearts.' And it does; but it goes in by our noses."

Mrs. Clifford had tacitly given her consent to Grace's copying the stories. This task was performed accordingly, much to the disgust of Horace, who declared that of the whole number only the tale of "Wild Robin" was worth reading.

"And 'Wild Robin,'" said Grace, instructively, "is the only one that has a moral for you, Horace. When our soldiers are starving so, it is really dreadful to see how you dislike corned beef and despise vegetables! Such a dainty boy as you needs to be stolen a while by the fairies."

"Well, Gracie, I reckon you'd run double-quick to pull me off the milk-white steed.

You couldn't get along without me two days. Look here! what story has a moral for you, miss? It's the 'Water-kelpie.' You are like the man that married Moneta: you're always wanting money."

"But it's for the soldiers, Horace," said Grace, with a smile of forbearance toward her brother. "I'm willing to give all my pocket-money; and I mean the other girls shall. If we're stingy to our country these days, we ought to be shot! 'Princess Hilda's' the best story in the book. I wish Isa Harrington could read it! She wouldn't make any more mischief between Cassy and me!"

"I like 'The Lost Sylphid' the best," said Prudy; "but *was* she a great butterfly, do you s'pose? The stories are all just as nice; just like book stories. I shouldn't think anybody made 'em up. Aunt 'Ria can write as

2

good as the big girls to the grammar-school. I promised not to believe a single word ; and I sha'n't. I'm glad she called it *my* Fairy Book."

CRISTOBAL.

A CHRISTMAS LEGEND.

LONG ago, in fair Burgundy, lived a lad named Cristobal. His large dark eyes lay under the fringe of his lids, full of shadows; eyes as lustrous as purple amethysts, and, alas! as. sightless.

He had not always been blind, as perhaps a wild and passionate lad, named Jasper, might have told you. On a certain Christmas Eve, a merry boy was little Cristobal, as he pattered along to church, trying with his wooden shoes to keep time to the dancing bells. In his hand he carried a Christmas candle of various colors. Never, he thought, was a rainbow so exquisitely tinted as that candle. Carefully he watched it when it winked its sleepy eye, eagerly begging his mamma to snuff it awake again. How gayly the streets twinkled with midnight lanterns! And how mortifying to the stars to be out-done by such a grand illumination!

A new painting had just been hung in the church,— the Holy Child, called by the peo-ple "Little Jesus," with an aureola about his head. Cristobal looked at this picture with reverent delight; and, to his surprise, the Holy Child returned his gaze: wherever he went, the sweet, sorrowful eyes followed him. There was a wondrous charm in that plead-ing glance. Why was it so wistful? What had those deep eyes to say?

The air was cloudy with the breath of frankincense and myrrh. Deep voices and the heavy organ sounded chants and an-

thems. There were prayers to the coming
Messiah, and the sprinkling of holy water;
and, at last, the midnight mass was ended.

Then, in tumult and great haste, the people went home for merry-makings. Cristobal, eager to see what the Yule-log might
have in store for him, rushed out of the
church with careless speed, stumbling over a
boy who stood in his way,— the haughty, in-
solent Jasper. Jasper's beautiful Christmas-
candle was cracked in twenty pieces by his
fall.

"I'll teach you better manners, young
peasant!" cried he, rushing upon Cristobal
in a frenzy, and dealing fierce blows without
mercy or reason.

It was then that Cristobal's eyes went out
like falling stars. Their lustre and beauty
remained ; but they were empty caskets,
their vision gone.

Then followed terrible anguish; and all Cristobal's mother could do was to hold her boy in her arms, and soothe him by singing. At last the fever was spent; but the pain still throbbed on, and sometimes seemed to burn into Cristobal's brain. He cried out again and again, "What right had that fierce Jasper to spring upon me so? I meant him no harm; and he knew it. Oh, I would like to see him chained in a den! He is like the wicked people who are turned into wolves at Christmas-tide. I would cry for joy if I could hear him groan with such pain as mine!".

Poor Cristobal never hoped to see again. He carried in his mind pictures of cities and hamlets, of trees, flowers, and old familiar faces; but oftenest came Jasper's face, just as it had last glared on him with blood-thirsty eyes. It was a terrible countenance. Only one charm could dispel the horror, — the remembrance of the beautiful Child in the church. That picture blotted out every thing else. It was like the refrain in the Burgundy carols, "Noel, Noel," which comes again and again, and never tires of coming.

A whole year passed away. Cristobal's mother only prayed now that her boy might suffer less: she had ceased to pray for the healing of his blindness.

Now it was Christmas - tide again. Ever since Advent, people had been clearing their throats, and singing carols. They roasted chestnuts, drank white wine, and chanted praises of the "Little Jesus," who was soon to come, bringing peace on earth, good-will to men.

In the streets, one heard bagpipes and minstrels ; and, by the hearthstones, the music of the wandering piper. The children began to talk again of the Yule-log, and to wonder what gifts Noel would bring to place under each end of it; for these little folks, who have no stocking - saint like our Santa Claus, believe in another quite as good, who rains down sugar - plums in the night.

Everywhere there was a joyful bustle. Housewives were making ready their choicest dishes for the great Christmas - supper; fathers were slyly peeping into shop - windows, and children hoarding their sous and centimes for bonbons and comfits.

Everybody was merry but Cristobal; or so thought the lad. He had no money to spend, and little but pain for his holiday-cheer. A patch here and there in his worn clothes was the best present his thrifty mother was able to make; always excepting the little variegated taper, which few were too poor to buy.

Christmas Eve came. Family friends dropped in. The Yule-log was set on the fire with shouts and singing. "Oh that I could see these kind faces!" moaned Cristobal. "No doubt, Jasper's chestnuts are popping merrily; and his shoes will be full of presents. And here am I! My head aches, and my eye-balls burn."

He stole out of the room, and, throwing himself on a wicker bench, mused over his troubles in solitude. One might have supposed him sleeping; for how should one imagine that his beautiful eyes were of no manner of use, except when they were closed? When Cristobal said, "Let me see," he dropped his eye-lids; and what he saw then, no artist can paint.

On this night, a beautiful child appeared before him, as like the picture of the Little Jesus as if it had stepped out of its frame on the church-wall. Even the crimson and blue tints of the old painting were faithfully preserved; and every fold of the soft drapery was the very same.

"I saw you, Cristobal, when you came before me with your colored candle, one year ago."

"I knew it, I knew it!" cried Cristobal, clasping his hands in awe. "I saw your eyes follow me; and I never once turned but you were looking. They told me it was only a picture; but I said for that very reason your eyes were sorrowful,— you longed to be alive."

The child replied by a slight motion of the head; and the aureola trembled like sunlight on the water. The longer Cristobal gazed, the more courage he gathered. "Lovely vision," said he, "if vision you may be, —I have said to myself, I would gladly walk to

Rome with peas in my shoes, if I could know what you wished to say to me that Christmas night."

" Only this, little brother: Are you ready for Christmas?"

"Alas! no: I never am. I have only two sous in the world."

" Poor Cristobal! Yet, without a centime, one may be ready for Christmas."

" But I am so very unhappy!"

" You do indeed look sad, little brother: where is your pain?"

"In my eyes," moaned the boy, pouring out the words with a delightful sense of relief; for he was sure they dropped into a pitying heart. " Beloved little Jesus, let me tell you that since I saw you last I have been wickedly injured. Now I have always a pain in my eyes: there are two flames behind them, which burn day and night."

I grieve for you," said the Child with exquisite tenderness; "yet, dear boy, for all that, you might be ready for Christmas: but is there not also a pain throbbing and burning in your *heart?*"

"Oh, if you mean that, I am tossed up and down by vexation: I am full of hatred against that terrible Jasper. It was all about a miserable Christmas-candle he carried. I broke it by pushing him down. Tell me, was he right to fly at me like a wild beast? Ought he not to suffer even as I have suffered? Is it just, is it right, for the great man's son to put out a peasant boy's eyes, and be happy again?"

"Misguided Jasper!" said the Child solemnly; "let him answer for his own sin: judge not, little brother."

Cristobal hid his face in his hands, and wept for shame.

"Shall I give you ten golden words for a Christmas-gift? Will you hide them in your heart, and be happy?"

"I will," answered Cristobal.

"They are these," said the Child with a voice of wondrous sweetness: "Pray for them which despitefully use you and persecute you."

Cristobal repeated the words, a soft light stealing over his face. "I will remember," he said, looking up to meet the pleading eyes of the Child: but, lo! the whole face had melted into the aureola; nothing was left but light. Yet Cristobal was filled with a new joy; and, as he opened his eyes, his dream — if dream it were — changed, becoming as sweet and solemn as a prayer. It seemed to him that the roof of the cottage glittered with stars, and was no longer a roof, but the boundless sky; and, afar off, like remem-

bered music, a voice fell on his ear, "For if
ye forgive men their trespasses, your heavenly Father will also forgive you your trespasses."

Cristobal arose, and, although still blind,
walked in light. "It is the aureola which
has stolen into my heart," thought Cristobal.
"The pain and hate are all gone. Now I am
ready for Christmas. I wish I could help
poor Jasper, who has such a weight of guilt
to carry!"

Next day, "golden-sided" Burgundy saw
no happier boy than Cristobal. He walked
in the procession that night, carrying a candle whose light he could not see; but what
did it signify, since there was light in his
soul?"

Hark! In the midst of the Christmas-
chimes breaks the jangling of fire-bells. The
count's house is on fire! The sparks pour

out thicker and faster; tongues of flame leap to the sky; the bells clang hoarsely; the Christmas procession is broken into wild disorder; the wheels of the engine roll through the streets, unheard in the din.

Cristobal rushed eagerly toward the flames, but was pulled away by the people.

"We cannot drown the fire!" they cried: "the building must fall! Are the inmates all safe?"

"All, thank Heaven!" cried the count.

"No: *Jasper!* See, he waves his hand from the third story! Save him! save my boy!"

Jasper had set fire to a curtain with his fatal Christmas-candle. Now he raved and shouted in vain: no one would venture up the ladder.

"O Little Jesus," whispered Cristobal, "give light to my eyes, even as unto my soul! Let me save Jasper!"

At once the iron band fell from Cristobal's vision. He saw, and, at the same moment, felt a supernatural strength. He tore away from the restraining arms of the people; he rushed up the ladder, shouting, "In the name of the Little Jesus!" He reached the window, heedless of his scorched arms. "Jasper!" he cried, seizing the half-conscious boy, "be not afraid: I have the strength to carry you."

And down the ladder he bore him, step by step, through the crackling flames.

Jasper was revived; and the fainting Cristobal was borne through the streets in the arms of the populace.

"Wonder of wonders!" they all shouted.

"It was the Little Jesus," gasped Cristobal: "he opened my eyes; he guided me up the ladder, and down again!"

"Hallelujah!" was now the cry. "On the

birthday of our Lord, the blind receive their sight."

"It is a triumph of faith," said the saints reverently.

"A miracle," murmured the nuns, making the sign of the cross.

"Not a miracle," replied the wise doctors, after they had first consulted their books: "it is only the electrifying of the optic nerve."

But hardly any two could agree; and what was so mysterious at the time is no clearer now.

"Dear little Cristobal," sobbed the broken-hearted Jasper, "how could you forgive such a wicked boy as I?"

"It was very easy," replied Cristobal, "when once the Little Jesus called me 'brother,' and bade me pray for you."

"Oh that I could repay you for your won-

derful deed of love," said Jasper, through
his tears.

"Do not thank me," whispered Cristobal,
with a look of awe; "thank the Little Jesus.
And when he comes again next year, to ask
what feelings we hold in our hearts, let us
both be ready for Christmas."

WILD ROBIN.

A SCOTTISH FAIRY TALE.

In the green valley of the Yarrow, near the castle-keep of Norham, dwelt an honest, sonsy little family, whose only grief was an unhappy son, named Robin.

Janet, with jimp form, bonnie eyes, and cherry cheeks, was the best of daughters: the boys, Sandie and Davie, were swift-footed, brave, kind, and obedient; but Robin, the youngest, had a stormy temper, and, when his will was crossed, he became as reckless as a reeling hurricane. Once, in a passion, he drove two of his father's "kye," or cattle, down a steep hill to their death. He seemed not to care for home or kindred, and often pierced the tender heart of his mother with sharp words. When she came at night, and "happed" the bed-clothes carefully about his form, and then stooped to kiss his nut-brown cheeks, he turned away with a frown, muttering, "Mither, let me be."

It was a sad case with Wild Robin, who seemed to have neither love nor conscience.

"My heart is sair," sighed his mother, "wi' greeting over sich a son."

"He hates our auld cottage and our muckle wark," said the poor father. "Ah, weel! I could a'maist wish the fairies had him for a season, to teach him better manners.'"

This the gudeman said heedlessly, little knowing there was any danger of Robin's being carried away to Elf-land. Whether the fairies were at that instant listening under the eaves, will never be known; but it chanced, one day, that Wild Robin was sent across the moors to fetch the kye.

" I'll rin away," thought the boy: " 'tis
hard indeed if ilka day a great lad like me
must mind the kye. I'll gae aff; and they'll
think me dead."

So he gaed, and he gaed, over round swelling hills, over old battle-fields, past the roof-
less ruins of houses whose walls were
crowned with tall climbing grasses, till he
came to a crystal sheet of water, called St.
Mary's Loch. Here he paused to take
breath. The sky was dull and lowering; but
at his feet were yellow flowers, which shone,
on that gray day, like freaks of sunshine.

He threw himself wearily upon the grass,
not heeding that he had chosen his couch within a little mossy circle known as a " fairy's
ring." Wild Robin knew that the country
people would say the fays had pressed that
green circle with their light feet. He had
heard all the Scottish lore of brownies, elves,

will-o'-the-wisps, and the strange water-kel-
pies, who shriek with eldritch laughter. He
had been told that the queen of the fairies
had coveted him from his birth, and would
have stolen him away, only that, just as she
was about to seize him from the cradle, he
had *sneezed;* and from that instant the fairy-
spell was over, and she had no more control
of him.

Yet, in spite of all these stories, the boy
was not afraid; and if he had been informed
that any of the uncanny people were, even
now, haunting his footsteps, he would not
have believed it.

"I see," said Wild Robin, "the sun is
drawing his night-cap over his eyes, and
dropping asleep. I believe I'll e'en take a
nap mysel', and see what comes o' it."

In two minutes he had forgotten St. Mary's
Loch, the hills, the moors, the yellow flowers.

He heard, or fancied he heard, his sister Janet calling him home.

" And what have ye for supper ? " he muttered between his teeth.

" Parritch and milk," answered the lassie gently.

" Parritch and milk ! Whist ! say nae mair ! Lang, lang may ye wait for Wild Robin : he'll not gae back for oatmeal parritch ! "

Next a sad voice fell on his ear.

" Mither's ; and she mourns me dead ! " thought he ; but it was only the far-off village-bell, which sounded like the echo of music he had heard lang syne, but might never hear again.

" D'ye think I'm not alive ? " tolled the bell. " I sit all day in my little wooden temple, brooding over the sins of the parish."

" A brazen lie ! " cried Robin.

" Nay, the truth, as I'm a living soul !

Wae worth ye, Robin Telfer: ye think yersel' hardly used. Say, have your brithers softer beds than yours? Is your ain father served with larger potatoes or creamier buttermilk? Whose mither sae kind as yours, ungrateful chiel? Gae to Elf-land, Wild Robin; and dool and wae follow ye! dool and wae follow ye!"

The round yellow sun had dropped behind the hills; the evening breezes began to blow; and now could be heard the faint trampling of small hoofs, and the tinkling of tiny bridle-bells: the fairies were trooping over the ground. First of all rode the queen.

> " Her skirt was of the grass-green silk,
> Her mantle of the velvet fine;
> At ilka tress of her horse's mane
> Hung fifty silver bells and nine."

But Wild Robin's closed eyes saw nothing;

his sleep-sealed ears heard nothing. The
queen of faries dismounted, stole up to him,
and laid her soft fingers on his cheeks.

"Here is a little man after my ain heart,"
said she: "I like his knitted brow, and the
downward curve of his lips. Knights, lift
him gently, set him on a red-roan steed, and
waft him away to Fairy-land."

Wild Robin was lifted as gently as a brown
leaf borne by the wind; he rode as softly as
if the red-roan steed had been saddled with
satin, and shod with velvet. It even may be
that the faint tinkling of the bridle-bells
lulled him into a deeper slumber; for when
he awoke it was morning in Fairy-land.

Robin sprang from his mossy couch, and
stared about him. Where was he? He
rubbed his eyes, and looked again. Dreaming, no doubt; but what meant all these nim-
ble little beings bustling hither and thither

in hot haste? What meant these pearl-be-
decked caves, scarcely larger than swallows'
nests? these green canopies, overgrown with
moss? He pinched himself, and gazed again.
Countless flowers nodded to him, and
seemed, like himself, on tiptoe with curiosity,
he thought. He beckoned one of the busy,
dwarfish little brownies toward him.

"I ken I'm talking in my sleep," said the
lad; "but can ye tell me what dell is this,
and how I chanced to be in it?"

The brownie might or might not have
heard; but, at any rate, he deigned no reply,
and went on with his task, which was pound-
ing seeds in a stone mortar.

"Am I Robin Telfer, of the Valley of
Yarrow, and yet canna shake aff my silly
dreams?"

"Weel, my lad," quoth the queen of the
fairies, giving him a smart tap with her wand,

"stir yersel', and be at work; for naebody idles in Elf-land."

Bewildered Robin ventured a look at the little queen. By daylight she seemed somewhat sleepy and tired; and was withal so tiny, that he might almost have taken her between his thumb and finger, and twirled her above his head; yet she poised herself before him on a mullein-stalk, and looked every inch a queen. Robin found her gaze oppressive; for her eyes were hard and cold and gray, as if they had been little orbs of granite.

"Get ye to work, Wild Robin!"

"What to do?" meekly asked the boy, hungrily glancing at a few kernels of rye which had rolled out of one of the brownie's mortars.

"Are ye hungry, my laddie?" touch a grain of rye if ye dare! Shell these dry bains; and if so be ye're starving, eat as many as ye can boil in an acorn-cup."

With these words she gave the boy a with-ered bean-pod, and, summoning a meek little brownie, bade him see that the lad did not over-fill the acorn-cup, and that he did not so much as peck at a grain of rye. Then, glancing sternly at her unhappy prisoner, she withdrew, sweeping after her the long train of her green robe.

The dull days crept by, and still there seemed no hope that Wild Robin would ever escape from his beautiful but detested prison. He had no wings, poor laddie; and he could neither become invisible nor draw himself through a keyhole bodily.

It is true, he had mortal companions: many chubby babies; many bright-eyed boys and girls, whose distracted parents were still seeking them, far and wide, upon the earth. It would almost seem that the wonders of Fairy-land might make the little prisoners happy. There were countless treasures to be had for the taking, and the very dust in the little streets was precious with specks of gold: but the poor children shivered for the want of a mother's love; they all pined for the dear home-people. If a certain task seemed to them particularly irksome, the heartless queen was sure to find it out, and oblige them to perform it, day after day. If they disliked any article of food, that, and no other, were they forced to eat, or starve.

Wild Robin, loathing his withered beans and unsalted broths, longed intensely for one little breath of fragrant steam from the toothsome parritch on his father's table, one glance at a roasted potato. He was homesick for the gentle sister he had neglected, the rough brothers whose cheeks he had pelted black and blue; and yearned for the very chinks in the walls, the very thatch on the home-roof.

Gladly would he have given every fairy-flower, at the root of which clung a lump of gold ore, if he might have had his own coverlet "happed" about him once more by the gentle hands he had despised.

"Mither," he whispered in his dreams, "my shoon are worn, and my feet bleed; but I'll soon creep hame, if I can. Keep the parritch warm for me."

Robin was as strong as a mountain-goat; and his strength was put to the task of threshing rye, grinding oats and corn, or drawing water from a brook.

Every night, troops of gay fairies and plodding brownies stole off on a visit to the upper world, leaving Robin and his companions

in ever deeper despair. Poor Robin! he
was fain to sing, —

> " Oh that my father had ne'er on me smiled!
>   Oh that my mother had ne'er to me sung!
> Oh that my cradle had never been rocked,
>   But that I had died when I was young!"

Now, there was one good-natured brownie
who pitied Robin. When he took a journey
to earth with his fellow-brownies, he often
threshed rye for the laddie's father, or
churned butter in his good mother's dairy,
unseen and unsuspected. If the little creature had been watched, and paid for these
good offices, he would have left the farm-
house forever in sore displeasure.

To homesick Robin he brought news of
the family who mourned him as dead. He
stole a silky tress of Janet's fair hair, and
wondered to see the boy weep over it; for

brotherly affection is a sentiment which never yet penetrated the heart of a brownie. The dull little sprite would gladly have helped the poor lad to his freedom, but told him that only on one night of the year was there the least hope, and that was on Hallow-e'en, when the whole nation of fairies ride in procession through the streets of earth.

So Robin was instructed to spin a dream, which the kind brownie would hum in Janet's ear while she slept. By this means the lassie would not only learn that her brother was in the power of the elves, but would also learn how to release him.

Accordingly, the night before Hallow-e'en, the bonnie Janet dreamed that the long-lost Robin was living in Elf-land, and that he was to pass through the streets with a cavalcade of fairies. But, alas! how should even

a sister know him in the dim starlight, among
the passing troops of elfish and mortal ri-
ders? The dream assured her that she
might let the first company go by, and the
second; but Robin would be one of the
third : —

" First let pass the black, Janet,
   And syne let pass the brown;
  But grip ye to the milk-white steed,
   And pull the rider down.

For *I* ride on the milk-white steed,
   And aye nearest the town :
Because I was a christened lad
   They gave me that renown.

My right hand will be gloved, Janet;
   My left hand will be bare;
And these the tokens I give thee:
   No doubt I will be there.

4

They'll shape me in your arms, Janet,
  A toad, snake, and an eel
But hold me fast, nor let me gang,
  As you do love me weel.

They'll shape me in your arms, Janet,
  A dove, bat, and a swan :
Cast your green mantle over me,
  I'll be myself again."

The good sister Janet, far from remembering any of the old sins of her brother, wept
for joy to know that he was yet among the living. She told no one of her strange dream;
but hastened secretly to the Miles Cross, saw
the strange cavalcade pricking through the
greenwood, and pulled down the rider on the
milk-white steed, holding him fast through all
his changing shapes. But when she had
thrown her green mantle over him, and
clasped him in her arms as her own brother

Robin, the angry voice of the fairy queen
was heard : —

   ‘ Up then spake the queen of fairies,
      Out of a bush of rye,
   ‘ You’ve taken away the bonniest lad
      In all my companie.

   ‘ Had I but had the wit, yestreen,
      That I have learned to-day,
   I’d pinned the sister to her bed
      E’re he’d been won away!’ ”

However, it was too late now. Wild Robin
was safe, and the elves had lost their power
over him forever. His forgiving parents
and his leal-hearted brothers welcomed him
home with more than the old love.

So grateful and happy was the poor laddie,
that he nevermore grumbled at his oat-meal
parritch, or minded his kye with a scowling
brow.

But to the end of his days, when he heard mention of fairies and brownies, his mind wandered off in a mizmaze. He died in peace, and was buried on the banks of the Yarrow.

THE VESPER STAR.

ONCE upon a time, the new moon was shining like a silver bow in the heavens, and the stars glittered and trembled as if they were afraid.

"What frightens you?" said the placid Moon; "be calm, like me."

"I am freezing," answered the North Star; "that is why I shake."

"We are dancing," said the Seven Sisters; "and, watch as closely as you please, you can never get a fair peep at our golden sandals, our feet twinkle so."

"I am sleepy," grumbled the Great Bear; "I am trying to keep my eyes open. Perhaps that is the reason I wink so much."

Thus, with one accord, they made excuses to the pale Moon, who is their guardian,—all but the sweet Vesper Star: she was silent; and when a white cloud floated by, she was glad of an excuse to hide her face.

"Let the North Star shiver, and the Seven Sisters dance, and all the golden stars hold a revel," thought she; "as for me, I am sad."

For you must know that the Vesper Star has a task to perform, and is not allowed to sleep. She keeps vigil over the Earth, by night; and never ceases her watch till the world is up in the morning. For the sick and sad, who cannot sleep, she feels an unutterable pity, so that her heart is always throbbing with sorrow.

The Moon looked at the Vesper Star, and said, "Dream on, sweet sister; for you, the noblest of all, have told me no falsehood."

This the Moon said because she knew that

none of the stars had given a true reason for twinkling so gayly that night. The truth was, they were filled with envy, and were trying to be as brilliant as possible, to compete with a flaming Comet which had just appeared in the sky.

It is not for man to know how long and how peacefully the gentle stars had travelled together, doing the work which God has appointed, without a murmur. But now that this distinguished stranger had arrived, the whole firmament was in dismay. How proudly he strode the heavens! how his blaze illumined the sky! The Stars whispered one to another, and cast angry eyes on the shining wonder.

"Make way for me," he said, sweeping after him a glorious train of light.

"Not I," muttered the fiery Mars.

"Not I," quoth the majestic Jupiter; "I do not move an inch."

The Comet flashed with a lofty disdain.

"Puny Stars," said he, "keep your places, give out all your light, — nobody heeds you; the place of honor is always by the Vesper Star; here I make my throne."

The Vesper Star smiled sadly, but without a twinge of envy.

"Welcome, shining one! Warm me with your fires; let us work together."

"Work!" cried the Comet, throwing out sparkles of scorn; "I was not born to work, but to *shine!*"

"Indeed!" said the Vesper Star; "you have come into strange company, then; for here we all work with a good will." "He does not burn with the true fire," thought the good Star; and she wrapped herself about with a soft cloud, and said no more.

"Oh that I could be set on fire like the Comet!" thought the cold North Star. "I would gladly burn to death if I could astonish the world with my blaze!"

"Let us die!" said the Seven Sisters; "let us die together; we have ceased to be noticed."

"Ah, hum!" growled the Great Bear; "so many years as I have kept watch in this sky; and now to be set one side by this upstart of a foreigner! I've a great mind to go to sleep and never wake up!"

"Hush!" whispered the Vesper Star gently; "do your duty, and trust God for the rest."

And lo! that very night there was an end of the Comet's splendor.

"Adieu, my dull friends," said he; "I am tired of a quiet life: a little more, and I should fade out entirely!"

Then, with a blaze and a whiz, and a dizzy wheel, he flashed out of the sky; and no one knew whither he went, or whence he came, any more than the path of the quick lightning.

The stars were ashamed of their envy, and went to their old work with a stronger will and a steadier purpose : but to the Vesper Star was given a brighter and sweeter light than to any other, because she had done her work without envy and without repining.

THE WATER–KELPIE.

Once there lived under the earth a race of fairies called gnomes. They were strange little beings, with dull eyes and harsh voices; but they did no harm, and lived in peace.

They never saw the sun; but they had lamps much brighter than our gaslight, which burned night and day, year after year.

They had music; but it was the tinkling of silver bells and golden harps, — not half so sweet as the singing of birds and the babbling of brooks.

Flowers they had none, but plenty of gems, — "the stars of earth." There were green trees in the kingdom: but the leaves were hard emeralds; and the fruit, apples of gold or cherries of ruby; and these precious gems the gnomes ground to powder, and swallowed with much satisfaction.

They heaped up piles of gold and dia-monds as high as your head; and never was there a gnome so poor as to build a house of any thing a whit coarser than jasper or onyx. You would have believed yourself dreaming, if you could have walked through the streets of their cities. They were paved with rosy almandine and snowy alabaster; and the pal-aces glittered in the gay lamplight like a million stars.

These gnomes led, for the most part, rather dull lives. Like their cousins, the water-sprites, or undines, they were roguish and shrewd, but had no higher views of life than our katydids and crickets. Indeed, they hardly cared for any thing but frisking about, eating and sleeping. But, after all, what can be expected of creatures without souls? One sees, now and seen, stupid human beings, whose eyes have no thoughts in them, and whose souls seem to be sound asleep. Such lumps of dulness might almost as well be gnomes, and slip into the earth and have done with it.

These underground folk had a great horror of our world. They knew all about it; for one of them had peeped out and taken a bird's-eye view. He went up very bravely, but hurried back with such strange accounts, that his friends considered him a little insane.

" Listen !" said the gnome, whose name was Clod. ' " The earth has a soft carpet, of a new kind of emerald; overhead is a blue roof, made of turquoise ; but I am told that there is a crack in it, and sometimes water comes pouring down in torrents. But the worst plague of all is a great glaring eyeball of fire, which mortals call the sun."

When Clod told his stories of the earth, he always ended by saying, —

" Believe me, it is bad luck to have the sun shine on you. It nearly put my eyes out ; and I have had the headache ever since."

Now, there was a young girl, named Moneta, who listened very eagerly to the old gnome's stories of the earth, and thought she would like to see it for herself. She was a kind little maiden, as playful as a kitten ; and her friends were not willing she should go. But Moneta had somewhere heard that fairies who marry mortals receive the gift of a human soul: so, in spite of all objections, she was resolved to take the journey ; for she had in her dark mind some vague aspirations after a higher state of being.

Then the gnome-family declared, that, if she once went away, they would never allow her to return; for they highly disapproved of running backward and forward between the two worlds, gossiping.

"Have you no love of country," cried they, "that you would willingly cast your lot among silly creatures who look down upon your race?"

The old gnome, who had travelled, took the romantic maiden one side, and said, —

"My dear Moneta, since you *will* go, I must tell you a secret; for you remember I have seen the world, and know all about it. Mortals are a higher race than ourselves, it is true; but that is only because they live atop o' the earth, while we are under their feet. They make a great parade about their little ticking jewel they call Conscience; but, after all, they will any of them sell it for one of our ear-rings! I assure you they love money better than their own souls; and I would advise you, as a friend that has seen the world, to load yourself with as much gold as you can carry."

So Moneta donned a heavy dress of spun gold, which was woven in such a manner, that, at every motion she made, it let fall a shower of gold-dust. She filled the sleeves with sardonyx, almandine, and amethyst; and hid in her bosom diamonds and sapphires enough to purchase a kingdom.

Then she went up a steep ladder, and knocked on the alabaster ceiling, using the charm which the gnome had given her: —

"Mother Earth, Mother Earth, set me free!"

At her words there was a sound as of an earthquake, and a little space was made, just large enough for her to crawl through.

When she had reached the top, the earth closed again, and she was left seated upon a rock; and the light of the sun was so dazzling, that she hid her face in her hands.

Thus she sat for a long time, not knowing whither to go, till a young man chanced to come that way, who said, " What do you here ? "

She raised her face at his words, and could not speak, so great was her surprise at the beauty of the strange youth. He, for his part, could not help smiling; for she was as yellow as an orange ; and an uglier little creature he had never beheld: but he said in a kind voice, —

" Come with me to my mother's house, and you shall be refreshed with cake and wine."

She arose to follow him ; and, as she walked, a bright shower of gold-dust sprinkled the earth at every step.

The young man held out his hands eagerly to catch the shining spray, thinking he would like such a rarely-gifted damsel for his wife; and, in truth, he smiled so sweetly, and dropped such winning words, that in time he won her heart and she became his bride.

> "And, when she cam' into the kirk,
>   She shimmered like the sun ;
>   The belt that was about her waist
>   Was a' with pearles bedone."

So great was her love for him, that she forgot her lost home under the earth; and every day, when she bade her husband "good-morning," she placed in his hand a precious stone; and he kissed her, calling her his "dear Moneta," his "heart's jewel." But at last the diamonds, sapphires, and rubies were all gone; and she was also losing the power of shedding gold-dust. Then her husband frowned on her, and no longer called her his "heart's jewel," or his "dear Moneta."

At length she presented him with a little daughter as lovely as a water-sprite, with hair like threads of gold. Now the father watched the babe with a greedy eye; for its mother had wept precious tears of molten gold before she received the gift of human grief, and he hoped her child would do the same; but, when he found it was only a common mortal, he shut his heart against the babe. Moneta was no longer yellow and ugly, but very beautiful; with deep eyes, out of which looked a sweet soul: yet she had lost her fairy gifts, and her husband had ceased to love her. The good woman mourned in secret; and would have wished to die, only her precious child comforted her heart.

One day, as she was sitting by the shore of the lake, a water-kelpie saw her weeping, and came to her in the form of a white-haired old man, saying, —

"Charming lady! why do you weep? Come with me to my kingdom under the waters. My people are always happy."

Then she looked where he bade her, and saw, afar down under the waters, a beautiful city, whose streets were paved with red and white coral.

The kelpie said, "Will you go down?"

"No," sighed Moneta, thinking of the kind words her husband had sometimes spoken to her: "I cannot go yet."

But the kelpie came every day, repeating the question, "Will you go now?" and she answered, "I cannot go yet."

But at last her husband said, —

"How often the thought comes to me, If

I had no wife and child, all this gold would be mine!" and he knitted his brows with a frown.

Then Moneta looked in his face, and said, —

"Dear Ivan, I have loved you truly; but you no longer care for Moneta. I will go away with the little child, and all our gold shall be yours. Farewell!"

Then she embraced him with falling tears. His heart was stirred within him; and he would have followed her, only he knew not which way she had gone.

Soon the water-kelpie came to him in the form of a horse; and ran before him, neighing fiercely, and breathing fire from his mouth. This is the way kelpies take to announce the fact that some one has gone under the water.

So the man followed the kelpie. His heart

was swelling with grief; and all his love for his wife and child had come back to him.

He looked into the lake, and saw the fair city. In a transparent palace Moneta was sitting, crowned with pearls, the child sleeping on her bosom. He shouted, —

"Come back, O Moneta!" but she heard him not.

He went every day to the same spot, never leaving it until the water was clear, and he had seen his wife and child. He cared no more for his fine castle and his gold; for the castle was empty, and the gold could not speak.

"Alas," cried he, "if I could listen to the music of Moneta's voice! if I could hold the child in my arms once more!"

Now he cared for nothing but to gaze into the waters at Moneta and her child.

One day, the water-kelpie appeared to him in the form of an old man.

THE WATER-KELPIE.   Page 70.

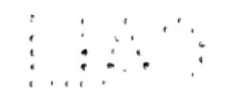

"Why sit you here, sighing like the north wind?" said the kelpie.

"I have loved gold better than my best friends," replied Ivan; "and now my best friends are taken away from me, and the gold is left; but I love it no longer."

"Ah, ah!" growled the kelpie; "I have heard of such men as you: nothing is dear till it is missed. You should have thought of that before. If your lost ones were to return, you would treat them as badly as ever, no doubt."

"No no," groaned Ivan; "I would love them better than all the wealth in the world! I would love them better than my own life! Ah, the sting it is to think of my own ingratitude!"

"Hold!" said the kelpie: "grumble to yourself if you like, but don't vex my ears with your complaints. Suppose I were to bring back Moneta and the child, — would you give me your chests of gold?"

"That I will," cried the man, "right joyfully."

"Not so fast: will you give me your castle as well?"

"Ah, yes, castle and gold; take them, and welcome."

"Not so fast: Moneta and her child are worth more than these. Will you give me the castle and gold, and ten years of your life?"

"With all my heart."

"Then," said the kelpie "go home, and to-morrow you shall see Moneta and her child."

When the morrow came, the husband and wife wept for joy at meeting once more; and Ivan said, —

"Can you forgive me, dearest Moneta?"

Moneta had already forgiven him; and the three — father, mother, and child — loved one another, and were content to the end of their lives ; and Ivan said, —

"Once for all I have found that gold cannot make one happy; but, with the blessing of a clear conscience, warm hearts and loving words are the sweetest things in life."

THE LOST SYLPHID.

"I tell the tale as 'twas told to me."

I HAVE heard that one night, on a distant shore, a band of water-nixies were dancing to gentle music, their golden sandals twinkling like stars.

A lord and lady were walking on the same shore. The lord's eyes were bent on the ground; but his wife paused, and said, —

"Listen, my lord, to that enchanting music!"

"I hear no music," he replied, laughing. "You must wake up, dear wife.

"With half-shut eyes, ever you seem
Falling asleep in a half-dream.'"

"But, my lord, those exquisite beings in gossamer robes! surely you see them!"

"I see the play of the moonbeams, my love, and nothing more."

But the wife stood transfixed. One beautiful fairy, taller and fairer than her companions, had wings, and floated through the dance, scarcely touching the earth.

"Was ever such a vision of lovliness?" cried the enraptured lady: "she must be my own little daughter,— eat of my bread, and sleep upon my bosom."

Then, kneeling, she sang,—

"Fair little nixies, that dwell near the water,
  Give me the winged one to be my own daughter."

The dance ceased. The nixies, bewildered, looked north and south, and knew not which way to flee; but the winged fairy, attracted by the human love in the lady's

eyes, glided slowly forward. Then the nixies stormed in fierce wrath, their willowy
figures swaying to and fro as if blown by the
wind.

"They shall not harm you, little one.
Come with me, be my own daughter, and I
will carry you home."

"Home!" echoed the lovely child; "my
home is in the Summer-land. Oh, will you
indeed carry me there?"

Then she folded her white wings, and
nestled in the lady's bosom like a gentle
dove, and was borne to a beautiful castle that
overlooked the sea. The water-nixies soon
forgot her, for they could not hold her mem-
ory in their little humming-bird hearts.

She was not of their race. Her wings
were soft and transparent, like those of a
white butterfly; and she ever declared that
she had once alighted from a cloud, and been

caught in a nixie's net spread upon the grass.

But, in time, her wings dwindled and disappeared; and then the lord, who was now her father, could not remember that she had ever been other than an earthly child.

"You fancy you were once a sylphid," said he; "but there are no sylphids, my sweet one, and there is no Summer-land."

The child became as dear to the lord and lady as their very heart's blood; and they forgot her foreign birth, and almost believed, as all the world did, that she was their own little daughter. But the child did not forget. She longed for the true home she had left; but whither should she go to seek it?

"Dear papa," said she, one day, "I beg you will not say again there are no sylphids; for I remember so well how I spread my wings and flew. It was glorious to see the clouds float under my feet!"

"Very well," said the lord; "if you like, I will say there are sylphids in the air, and trolls inside the earth; and, once on a time, I was myself a great white butterfly: do you remember chasing me over a bed of roses?"

"O papa, now you laugh! I love the twinkle in your eye; and I am so glad it is you, and no one else, who is my papa; but just the same, and forevermore, I shall keep saying, *I was a sylphid!*"

Sometimes, when she set her white teeth into some delicious fruit, she said with dreamy eyes, —

"These grapes of Samarcand came across the seas; but they are not so sweet as the fruit in my own garden, mamma."

"And where is your garden, my child?"

" Oh, in the Summer-land. I always forget

that you have never seen it. When I go there again, mamma, I will certainly take you too; for I love you with all my heart. I can never go without you."

When she heard the evening-bells from the minster, she said, " Oh, they are like the joy-bells at home, only not so sweet. Nothing, here, is so sweet. Even my dear mamma is not so lovely as the lady who comes when I am asleep."

Little One — they called her Little One for the want of a name — loved to prattle about the wonders of that mysterious fairy-land, which no one but herself had ever seen. Her mother would not check her, but let her tell her pretty visions of remembered rainbows, and palaces, and precious gems. She said, —

" The child has such a vivid fancy! It is not all of us who can see pictures when our eyes are shut."

But the lord was not so well pleased; and once, when his daughter looked at a frozen stream and murmured, " *We* have the *happiest* rivers at home; they sing all day long, all the year, without freezing! Can I find that Summer-land again! Oh, I would creep all over the world to seek it," he replied,—

"Little One, it is some cloud-city you are thinking of, some dream-land, or isle of Long Ago, which you will never see again. I beg you to forget these wild fancies."

But still the child dreamed on. Once she heard the glad song of the Hyperboreans:—

> "I come from a land in the sun-bright deep,
>   Where golden gardens glow;
>   Where the winds of the North, becalmed in sleep,
>   Their conch-shells never blow."

She clapped her hands, murmuring to herself,—

" *There* is my home! I think I remember now it *was* 'a land in the sun-bright deep!'"

So, when she journeyed with her parents to distant countries, she always hoped that some ship would bear her away to the Happy Isles; and when they once touched a bright shore, and some one cried, "The isles of Greece! the isles of Greece!" she thought she was home at last, and hardly dared look at the remembered shore. But, alas, she had not yet reached the Summer-land: this was not her home.

Then she heard her father say that the jewels she wore had been brought up from the deep places under the earth.

"I wonder I had not thought of that," she said to herself. "Since there are such beautiful gems in my lost home, it must lie under the earth. No doubt if I could only find the right cave, and walk in it far enough' I should come to the Summer-land."

So she set out, one day, in wild haste, but only lost herself in a deep cavern; and, when she found daylight again, she was all alone upon the face of the earth. Her father and mother were nowhere to be seen. She shouted their names, and ran to and fro seeking them till her strength was all spent. It was growing dark; and Little One could only creep under a shelter, and weep herself asleep.

Next morning it was no better, but far worse. Her wretched parents had gone home, believing her drowned in the sea. Poor Little One was now all alone in the world, and her heart ached with the cold. Kind friends gave her food and shelter, and her clothing was warm as warm could be; still her heart ached with the cold. People praised her beauty so much that she dared not look up to let them see how lovely she was; but she had lost both her father and mother, and her heart ached and ached. She thought winter was coming on; and the world was growing so chilly, that now she must certainly set out for the Summer-land. Then she said, —

"If I am a sylphid, perhaps my home is over the hills, and far away. Yes: I think it must be in the country where the music goes."

For she thought, when she heard music, that it seemed to hover and float over the earth, and lose itself in the sky; so she began to set her face toward the country where the music goes. But, though she gazed till her eyes ached, she never saw her long-lost home, nor so much as a glimpse of one of its spires.

One night, after gazing and weeping till she could scarcely see, and had no tears left, the bright being who visited her dreams came and whispered, —

"If there be a land so fair
　O'er the mountain shining,
You will never enter there
　By looking up and pining."

"Dear me! then what shall I do?" said Little One, clasping her hands. "I am tired of the dropping rain, and the bleak winds; I have lost my father and mother; I long to go home to the Summer-land."

"There are hills to climb, and streams to cross," said the fairy.

"But I have stout shoes," laughed Little One.

"There are thorns and briers all along the road."

"But I can bear to be pricked."

"Then I will guide you," said the fairy.

"How can that be?" cried the child. "You come to me in dreams; but by daylight I cannot see so much as the tips of your wings."

"Listen, and you will hear my voice," replied the fairy. "Set out toward the East, at dawn, to-morrow, and I will be with you."

When Little One awoke, the sun was rising, and she said, —

"Oh that golden gate! The sun has left it open: do you see it, beautiful lady?"

"I see it," whispered the fairy: "I am close beside you."

"Then," said Little One, fastening her dress, and putting on all the jewels she could possibly carry, "I think I will set out at once; for, if I make all speed, I may reach the Summer-land before that golden gate is closed."

She pressed on, as the fairy directed, up a steep hill, her eyes fixed on the glowing eastern sky. But, as the sun strode up higher, the morning clouds melted away.

" Where is my golden gate ?" cried the child.

" Weeping so soon?" whispered the fairy.

" Do not scold me, dear Whisper," moaned the child; "you know I have lost my kind father and mother ; and the thorns prick me ; and then this is such a lonely road; there is nobody to be seen."

The truth was, there were children gathering strawberries on the hill, and old women digging herbs; but Little One did not see them, for she was all the while watching the sky. But she was soon obliged to pause, and take breath.

" Look about you," said the Whisper, " you may see some one as unhappy as yourself."

The child looked, and saw a little girl driving a goat; while large tears trickled down her cheeks, and moistened her tattered dress. For a moment, Little One's heart ceased aching with its own troubles.

"What is your name, little girl?" said she: "and why do you weep?"

"My name is Poor Dorel," replied the child; "my father and mother are long since dead; and I have nothing to eat but goat's milk and strawberries:" and, as she spoke, the large tears started afresh.

"Poor Dorel! you are the first one I ever saw who had as much trouble as I. I, too, have lost a father and mother."

"Were they a king and queen?" asked Dorel, wiping her eyes, and gazing at Little One's beautiful dress and glittering ornaments.

"They loved me dearly," replied Little

One sadly; "yet I never heard that they were king and queen. Come with me, darling Dorel!" I never before saw any one who was hungry. Come with me! I live in a country where there is food enough for everybody."

"Where is that?" said Dorel, eagerly.

" I do not quite know, little girl; but it is not in the bosom of the earth, and it is not in the sun-bright deep: so I suppose it is over the hills, and far away."

" Now I know who you are," said Dorel. "You are the *lost sylphid;* and people say you have travelled all over the world. But, if you do not know the way home, pray how can you tell which road to take?"

"Oh! I have a guide, — a beautiful fairy, called Whisper: she shows me every step of the way. I wish you would go too, little Dorel!"

"I think I will not, little Sylphid; for, if you have only a Whisper for a guide, I do not believe you will ever get there; but, oh, you are very, very beautiful!"

"If you will not go," said Little One, "let me, at least, give you a few of my jewels: you can sell them for bread."

So saying, she took from her girdle some turquoise ornaments, and placed them in Dorel's hand with a kiss which had her whole heart in it.

"Now I love you," said Dorel; "but more for the kiss than any thing else; and I am going before you to cut down the thorns that shoot out by the wayside. I am a little mountain-girl, and know how to use the pruning-knife."

Little One danced for joy. She found she could now walk with wonderful ease; for not only were there no more sharp thorns to prick her, but her heart was also full of a new love, which made the whole world look beautiful.

"You see the way is growing easier," said the Whisper.

"Pour out thy love like the rush of a river,
  Wasting its waters forever and ever."

"So I will," said Little One. "Is there any one else to love?"

By and by she met an old woman, bent nearly double, and picking up dry sticks with trembling hands.

"Poor woman!" said Little One: "I am going to love you."

"Dear me!" said the old crone, dropping her sticks, and looking up with surprise in every wrinkle: "you don't mean *me?* Why, my heart is all dried up."

"Then you need to be loved all the more," cried Little One heartily.

The poor woman laughed; but, at the same time, brushed a tear from her eye with the corner of her apron.

"I thought," said Little One, "I was the only unhappy one in the world: it seemed a pity my heart should ache so much; but, oh, I would rather have it ache than be dried up!"

"I suppose you never were beaten," said the old woman; "you were never pelted with whizzing stones?"

"Indeed I never, never was!" replied Little One, greatly shocked by the question.

"By your costly dress, I know you never were so poor as to be always longing for food. Let me tell you, my good child, when one is beaten and scolded, and feels cold all winter, and hungry all summer, it is no wonder one's heart dries up!"

Little One threw her arms about the old

woman's neck. "Let me help you pick sticks!" said she; "you are too old for hard work; your hands tremble too much."

Swiftly gathering up a load of fagots, she put them together in a bundle.

"Now, how many jewels shall I give her?" thought the child. "She must never want for food again."

"How many?" echoed the Whisper.

"Give as the morning that flows out of heaven:
　Give as the free air and sunshine are given."

"Then she shall have half," said Little One in great glee. "Here, poor woman, take these sapphires and rubies and diamonds, and never be hungry again!"

"Heavenly child!" said the stranger, laying her wasted hand on the sylphid's bright head, and blessing her, "it is little except thanks that an old creature like me can give;

yet may be you will not scorn this pair of little shoes: they are strong, and, when you have to step on the sharp mountain-rocks, they will serve you well."

Little One's delicate slippers were already much worn, and she gladly exchanged them for the goat-skin shoes; but, strange to relate, no sooner had she done so than she found herself flitting over rocks and rough places with perfect ease, and at such speed, that, when she looked back, in a moment, she had already left the old woman far behind, and out of sight. They were magical shoes; but, no matter how fast they skimmed over the ground, Dorel, out of pure love, continued to go before, talking and laughing and smoothing the way.

One by one Little One sold her jewels to buy bread, which she shared with all the needy she chanced to meet. After many

days there remained but one gem ; and she
wept because she had no more to give. But,
through her tears, she now, for the first time,
fancied she could see the spires and turrets
of her beautiful home, though, as yet, very
far off.

"How fast I have come!" said she, laughing with delight. "But for these magical
shoes, and Dorel's pruning-knife, I should
have been even now struggling at the foot
of the hill."

Then she looked down at her torn dress.

"What a sad plight I am in! no one will
know me when I get home!"

"Never fear!" said the fairy: "you are
sure to be welcome."

Little One now held up her last jewel in
the sunlight, while a starving boy looked at
it with eager eyes.

"Take it!" said she, weeping with the ten-

THE LOST SYLPHID.   Page 95.

derest pity. "I only wish it were a diamond instead of a ruby, — a diamond as large as my heart!"

The boy blessed her with a tremulous voice. Little One pressed on, singing softly to herself, till she came to a frightful chasm, full of water.

"How shall I ever cross it!" she cried in alarm.

"May I help you, fair Sylphid?" said the grateful boy to whom she had given her last jewel. "I can make a bridge in the twinkling of an eye."

So saying, he threw across the roaring torrent a film which looked as frail as any spider's web.

"It will bear you," said the Whisper: "do not be afraid!"

So Little One ventured upon the gossamer bridge, which was to the eye as delicate as mist; but to the feet as strong as adamant. She hushed her fears, and walked over it with a stout heart.

Now, she was on the borders of the Summer-land. Here were the turrets and spires, the soft white clouds, the green fields, and sunny streams. Instantly her long-lost wings appeared again; and she spread them like a happy bird, and flew home. Oh, it was worth years of longing and pain! She was held in tender embraces, and kissed lovingly by well-remembered friends. To her great surprise and delight, her father and mother were both there they had arrived at the Summer-land while seeking their Little One.

"Now I know," said her father, "that my daughter was not dreaming when she longed for her remembered home."

Little One looked at her soiled dress; but the stains had disappeared; and, most wonderful! all the jewels she had worn on her neck and arms, and in her girdle, were there yet, burning with increased brilliancy. Little One gazed again, and counted to see if any were missing. Yes: two she had sold for bread were not there. It was the jewels she had *given away* which had come back in some mysterious manner and were more resplendent than before.

"Ah!" said she, with a beaming smile, "now I know what it means when they say, 'All you give, you will carry with you.' It was delightful to scatter my gems by the wayside; but I did not think they would all be given back to me when I reached home!"

Then, intwining arms with a bright sylphid, she flew with her over the gardens in a trance of delight.

"Here," said Little One, "is my own dear garden. I remember the border and the

7

paths right well; but it never bore such
golden fruit, it never glowed with such beautiful flowers."

" Your fairy, the one you call Whisper, has
taken care of it for your sake," said the
sister sylphid. " Do you know that those
flowers, and those trees with fruit like ' bonny beaten gold,' have been watered by your
tears, Little One ? It is in this way they
have attained their matchless beauty and
grace."

" *My tears*, little sister ? "

" Yes, your tears. Every one you shed
upon earth, your fairy most carefully preserved ; and see what wonders have been
wrought ! "

" If I had known that," said Little One
clapping her hands, " I would have been *glad*
of all my troubles ! I would have smiled
through my tears ! "

Now I know no more than I have told of this story of the Lost Sylphid. I tell the tale as 'twas told to me ; and I wish, with all my heart, it were true.

THE CASTLE OF GEMS.

Once upon a time, though I cannot tell
when, and in what country I do not now remember, there lived a maiden as fair as a
lily, as gentle as a dewdrop, and as modest
as a violet. A pure, sweet name she had, —
it was Blanche.

She stood one evening, with her friend
Victor, by the shore of a lake. Never had
the youth or maiden seen the moonlight so
enchanting; but they did not know

> " It was midsummer day,
>   When all the fairy people
>   From elf-land come away."

Presently, while they gazed at the lake,
which shone like liquid emerald and sapphire

and topaz, a boat, laden with strangely beautiful beings, glided towards them across the
waters. The fair voyagers were clad in
robes of misty blue with white mantles
about their waists, and on their heads
wreaths of valley-lilies.

They were all as fair as need be; but fair-
est of all was the helms-woman, the queen of
the fairies. Her face was soft and clear like
moonlight; and she wore a crown of nine
large diamonds, which refracted the evening
rays, and formed nine lunar rainbows.

The fairies were singing a roundelay; and,
as the melody floated over the waters, Victor
and Blanche listened with throbbing hearts.
Fairy music has almost passed away from the
earth; but those who hear it are strangely
moved, and have dreams of beautiful things
which have been, and may be again.

"It makes me think of the days of long

ago when there was no sin," whispered Blanche.

" It makes me long to be a hero," answered Victor with a sparkling eye.

All the while the pearly boat was drifting toward the youth and maiden; and, when it had touched the shore, the queen stepped out upon the land as lightly as if she had been made entirely of dewdrops.

" I am Fontana," said she; " and is this Blanche ? "

She laid her soft hand upon the maiden's shoulder; and Blanche thought she would like to die then and there, so full was she of joy.

" I have heard of thy good heart, my maiden : now what would please thee most ? " said the queen.

Blanche bowed her head, and dared not speak.

Queen Fontana smiled: when she smiled it was as if a soft cloud had slid away from the moon, revealing a beautiful light.

"Say pearls and diamonds," said Victor in her ear.

"I don't know," whispered Blanche: "they are not the best things."

"No," said the queen kindly: "pearls and diamonds are *not* the best things."

Then Blanche knew that her whisper had been overheard, and she hid her face in her hands for shame. But the queen only smiled down on her, and, without speaking, dropped into the ground a little seed. Right at the feet of Blanche, it fell; and, in a moment, two green leaves shot upward, and between them a spotless lily, which hung its head with modest grace.

Victor gazed at the perfect flower in wonder, and, before he knew it, said aloud, "Ah, how like Blanche!"

The queen herself broke it from the stem, and gave it to the maiden, saying, —

"Take it! it is my choicest gift. Till it fades (which will never be), love will be thine; and, in time to come, it will have power to open the strongest locks, and swing back the heaviest doors.

> 'Gates of brass cannot withstand
> One touch of this magic wand.'"

Blanche looked up to thank the queen; but no words came, — only tears.

"I see a wish in thine eyes" said Fontana.

"It is for Victor," faltered Blanche, at last: "he wishes to be rich and great."

The queen looked grave.

"Shall I make him one of the great men of the earth, little Blanche? Then he may one day go to the ends of the world, and forget thee."

Blanche only smiled, and Victor's cheek flushed.

"I shall be a great man," said he, — "perhaps a prince; but, where I go, Blanche shall go: she will be my wife."

"That is well," said the queen: "never forget Blanche, for her love will be your dearest blessing."

Then, removing from her girdle a pair of spectacles, she placed them in the youth's hand. He drew back in surprise. "Does she take me for an old man?" thought he. He had expected a casket of gems at least; perhaps a crown.

"Wait," said Fontana: "they are the eyes of Wisdom. When you have learned their use, you will not despise my gift. Keep a pure heart, and always remember Blanche. And now farewell!"

So saying, she moved on to the boat, floating over the ground as softly as a creeping mist.

When Blanche awoke next morning, her first thought was, " Happy are the maidens who have sweet dreams ! " for she thought she had only been wandering in a midsummer's night's dream ; so, when she saw her lily in the broken pitcher where she had placed it, great was her delight. But a change had come over it during the night. It was no longer a common lily, — its petals were large pearls, and the green leaves were now green emeralds. This strange thing had happened to the flower, that it might never fade.

After this, people looked at Blanche, and said, " How is it? she grows fairer every day ! " and every one loved her; for the human heart has no choice but to love what is good and gentle.

As for Victor, he at first put on his spectacles with a scornful smile : but, when he had worn them a moment, he found them very wonderful things. When he looked through them, he could see people's thoughts written out on their faces; he could easily decipher the fine writing which you see traced on green leaves; and found there were long stories written on pebbles in little black and gray dots.

When he wore the spectacles, he looked so wise, that Blanche hardly dared speak to him. She saw that one day he was to become a great man.

At last Victor said he must leave his home, and sail across the seas. Tears filled the eyes of Blanche ; but the youth whispered, —

"I am going away to find a home for you and me : so adieu, dearest Blanche ! "

Now Victor thought the ship in which he sailed moved very slowly; for he longed to reach the land which he could see through his magic spectacles: it was a beautiful kingdom, rich with mines of gold and silver.

When the ship touched shore, the streets were lined with people who walked to and fro with sad faces. The king's daughter, a beautiful young maiden, was very ill; and it was feared she must die.

Victor asked one of the people if there was no hope.

It so happened that this man was the greatest physician in the kingdom and he answered, —

" Alas, there is no hope ! "

Then Victor went to a distant forest where he knew a healing spring was to be found. Very few remembered it was there ; and those who had seen it did not know of its power to heal disease.

Victor filled a crystal goblet with the precious water, and carried it to the palace. The old king shook his head sadly, but consented to let the attendants moisten the parched lips of the princess with the water, as it could do no harm. Far from doing harm, it wrought a great good; and, in time, the royal maiden was restored to health.

Then, for gratitude, the king would have given his daughter to Victor for a wife; but Victor remembered Blanche, and knew that no other maiden must be bride of his.

Not long after this, the king was lost overboard at sea during a storm. Now the people must have a new ruler. They determined to choose a wise and brave man; and, young as he was, no man could be found braver and wiser than Victor: so the people elected him for their king. Thus Fontana's gift of the eyes of Wisdom had made him truly " one of the great men of earth."

In her humble home, Blanche dreamed every night of Victor, and hoped he would grow good, if he did not become great; and Victor remembered Blanche, and knew that her love was his dearest blessing.

"This old palace," thought he "will never do for my beautiful bride."

So he called together his people, and told them he must have a castle of gems. Some of the walls were to be of rubies, some of emeralds, some of pearls. There was to be any amount of beaten gold for doors and pillars; and the ceilings were to be of milk-white opals, with a rosy light which comes and goes.

All was done as he desired; and, when the castle of gems was finished, it would need a pen of jasponyx dipped in rainbows to describe it.

Victor thought he would not have a guard

of soldiers for his castle, but would **lock** the four golden gates with a magic **key**, so that no one could enter unless the gates should swing back of their own accord.

When the castle of gems was just completed, and not a soul was in it, Victor locked the gates with a magic key, and then dropped the key into the ocean.

"Now," thought he, "I have done a wise thing. None but the good and true can enter my castle of gems. The gates will not swing open for men with base thoughts or proud hearts!"

Then he hid himself under the shadow of a tree, and watched the people trying to enter. But they were proud men, and so the gates would not open.

King Victor laughed, and said to himself, —

"I have done a wise thing with my magic

key. How safe I shall be in my castle of gems!"

So he stepped out of his hiding-place, and said to the people, —

"None but the good and true can get in."

Then he tried to go in himself; but the gates would not move.

The king bowed his head in shame, and walked back to his old palace.

"Alas!" said he to himself, "wise and great as I am, I thought *I* could go in. I see it must be because I am filled with pride. Let me hide my face; for what would Blanche say if she knew, that, because my heart is proud, I am shut out of my own castle? I am not worthy that she should love me; but I hope I shall learn of her to be humble and good."

The next day he sailed for the home of his childhood. When Blanche saw him, she blushed, and cast down her eyes; but Victor knew they were full of tears of joy. He held her hand, and whispered, —

"Will you go with me and be my bride, beautiful Blanche ? "

" I will go with you," she answered softly; and Victor's heart rejoiced.

All the while Blanche never dreamed that he was a great prince, and that the men who came with him were his courtiers. .

When they reached Victor's kingdom, and the people shouted "Long live the queen!" Blanche veiled her face, and trembled; for Victor whispered in her ear that the shouts were for her. And, as the people saw her beautiful face through her gossamer veil, they cried all the more loudly, —

" Long live Queen Blanche ! Thrice welcome, fair lady ! "

The sun was sinking in the west, and his

8

rays fell with dazzling splendor upon the castle of gems. When Blanche saw the silent, closed castle and its golden gates, she remembered the words of Queen Fontana, who had said that her lily should have power to "open the strongest locks, and swing back the heaviest doors."

Like one walking in a dream, she led Victor toward the resplendent castle. She touched, with her lily, the lock which fastened one of the gates.

> " Gates of gold could not withstand
> One touch of that magic wand."

In an instant, the hinges trembled; and the massive door swung open so far, that forty people could walk in side by side. Then it slowly closed, and locked itself without noise.

One of the people who passed in was the

king, whose heart was no longer proud. The others, who had entered unwittingly, could not speak for wonder. Some of them were poor, and some were lame or blind; but all were good and true.

At the rising of the moon a wonderful thing came to pass. The people entered the castle of gems, and became beautiful. This was through the power of the magic lily.

Now there were no more crooked backs and lame feet and sightless eyes; and the king looked at these people, who were beautiful as well as good, and declared he would have them live in the castle; and the gentlemen should be knights; and the ladies, maids of honor.

To this day Victor and Blanche rule the kingdom; and such is the charm of the lily, — so like the pure heart of the queen, — that the people are becoming gentle and good.

Until Queen Fontana shall call for the magic spectacles and the lily of pearl, it is believed that Victor and Blanche will live in the castle of gems, though the time should be a hundred years.

THE ELF OF LIGHT.

A NORSE TALE.

In the strange island of Iceland, thrown up, by fire, from the depths of the sea, there once lived a lad who worshipped the god Odin, and was taught from two absurd books called the Eddas. He wished to fight and die on a battle-field, so that his soul might cross a rainbow-bridge, and dwell in the beautiful halls of Valhalla. There — so the Eddas say — are the chosen heroes, who are forever fighting all day, and feasting all night.

Thus, instead of a Bible, young Thule studied wild fairy-tales; yet, for all his heathenish training, he had some noble traits, which a Christian lad might imitate.

He lived with his widowed mother at the edge of a forest. The snow piled itself in drifts, and the wind howled through the trees, and crept in at the windows; for the cottage was old, and a blind hurricane might almost have mistaken it for a heap of brush-wood. But Thule was quite as happy as if the hut had been a palace. He loved the winter-beauty of his mother's face, and the silvery hair half hidden under her black cap. All the fire they burned was made of the dry sticks he gathered in the forest, and more than half the money they used was earned by his small hands.

In one of the ice-months of the year, when the weather was sharper than a serpent's tooth, Thule came home from a hard day's work; and, the chillier he grew, the more he whistled to keep up a brave heart. Looking at the horizon before him, he saw the cold glare which we call Northern Lights, but which he knew to be the flickering of helmets and shields and spears.

"The warlike maidens are out to-night," thought the boy: "they are going to the battle-fields to decide who is worthy to be slain. How I love to see the sky lighted up with the flash of their armor! Odin, grant I may one day be a hero, and walk over the bridge of a rainbow!"

Then Thule went to his whistling again; but, just as he struck into the forest where the deep shadows lay, he heard a faint moan, which sounded like a human voice, or might have been a sudden gust of wind in a hollow tree.

"Perchance it is some poor creature even colder than I," thought the boy: "I hope not a *troll!*"

Hurrying to the spot whence the sound came, he found an ugly, long-nosed dwarf lying on the ground, nearly perishing with cold. It was growing late, and the boy himself was benumbed; but he went briskly to work, chafing the hands and face of the stranger, even taking off his own blue jacket to wrap it about the dwarf's neck.

"Poor old soul, you shall not die of cold!" said he; then, helping him to rise, he added cheerily, "We will go to my mother's cottage, and have a warm supper of oat-cakes and herrings; and our fire of dry boughs will do you good."

The noble boy knew there was barely supper enough for two, but did not mind going hungry to bed for charity's sake. In the ear of his heart, he heard the words of his mother: —

"Never fear starving, my son, but freely share your last loaf with the needy."

They walked through the forest, the old man leaning heavily on the youth's shoulder.

"Why should you befriend a poor wretch who cannot repay you?" whined the dwarf in a hollow voice which startled Thule, it was so like the echo sent back by a mountain or a rock.

"I do not ask or wish to be repaid," was the reply. "Don't you know what the proverb says? 'Do good, and throw it into the sea; if the fishes don't know it, Odin will!'"

"Yes: Odin shall know it, never fear," answered the dwarf; "but, as I happen to be informed that your tea-table is not quite large enough for three, I think I will decline your invitation to supper. Really, my lad," he continued, "it would delight me to do you a little favor; for, though I am only a poor dwarf, I know how to be grateful. By the way, have you seen such a thing hereabouts as a green alder-tree?"

"A green alder-tree in winter-time!" cried Thule.

"A curious thing, indeed," said the dwarf; "but I chanced to see one the other night in my rambles. Ah! look, here it is right before your eyes."

All the other forest-trees were dry and hard, their hearts frozen within them; but this tree was alive, hidden behind a clump of firs. When Thule began to dig about its roots, it seemed to come out of the ground of its own free will, and to lie over his shoulders as if it would caress him.

"Take home the little tree, and plant it before your door, my lad."

The youth turned to thank the stranger; but he had vanished. Then Thule ran home with all speed to tell his mother of the little old man who had faded from his sight like a wreath of smoke.

"Now I wonder what it is you have seen," said the good woman, raising her hands in surprise. "Was he brown, my son, with a long nose?"

"As brown as a nut, mother, with no end of nose."

"Just as I supposed, my child! That dwarf is a wonderful creature, — one of the night-elves, a race gifted with great understanding. Know, my son, that he carves runes upon stones; and he no doubt assisted in making Thor's hammer, that terrible instrument which can crush the skull of a giant."

"One thing I observed," said the boy: "he blinked at that flashing in the sky, which people call Northern Lights; he had to shade his eyes with his funny little hand."

"Did he, indeed? Poor Elf! Light is painful to his race; and I have even heard that a stroke of sunshine is able to turn them into stones. I am almost afraid of this little tree," added the good mother musingly. "You know what we read in the holy Eddas: Both the alder and the ash trees should be held sacred; for Odin formed man from the ash, and woman from the alder. Nevertheless, the night-elf could not have meant to do you a mischief. Let us plant the tree as he directed."

"What, in the frozen ground, under the snow?"

But it now, for the first time, appeared that there was a spot of earth near the south window, which must have been waiting for the tree, since it was as soft and warm as if the sun had been shining on it all the year. Here they planted the alder; and Thule brought water, and moistened the roots.

Next morning the tree seemed to have

grown a foot higher; and by daylight its leaves showed a silver lining.

"May Odin favor my pretty alder!" said Thule; "nor let the frost pinch it, nor the winds blacken its green buds!"

Thule went into the woods again; and, as he was whistling at his work, he happened to look down, and there, on the ground, at his feet, lay a purse, well lined with gold. He counted the pieces: fifty, all bright and new.

"I will go to the town," thought the boy, shaking his head and sighing (for the gold was very tempting), "I will go to the town, and ask who has lost a purse with fifty pieces of precious gold. Ah, me! I wish I could keep it!" then we should swim in herrings and oil; and who knows but, for once in my life, I might even get a taste of venison?"

But next moment he loosened his greedy clutch at the purse. "No matter how bravely it shines! it is not *my* gold; and it is too heavy for me to carry. Stolen money is worse than a mill-stone about one's neck, so my mother says."

"Keep the purse, little boy," said a sweet voice close by his elbow. He turned, and saw a beautiful child, as radiant as a sunbeam, and clad in garments of delicate and transparent texture.

"I will be your friend, little boy. That purse was dropped by a lady who wears a fur cloak and long veil. If she asks for her treasure, I can say it fell into a hole in the ground. Everybody believes me: never fear!"

"Poor misguided angel!" said the boy, amazed by her wondrous beauty no less than by her apparent want of truth. "You are, indeed, a lovely little tempter; but I have a dear mother at home, and I love her better than a million pieces of gold. I must go to the town, and seek out this lady you mention, who wears a fur cloak and long veil."

"Nay, if you will be so stupid," said the shining child, "why, I will even go with you, and show you the way."

So, gliding gracefully before the bewildered youth, she led him out of the forest, into the most crowded part of the city, up to the door of a splendid mansion; but, when Thule turned his head only an instant, she was gone, and no trace of her was to be seen: she seemed to have melted into sunshine.

The lady of the house received the purse with thanks, and would gladly have given Thule a piece of the gold; but, much as the boy longed for it, he put it aside, saying, "No, madam: my mother assures me I must be honest without the hope of reward. She

would not like me to take wages for not being a thief!"

The next morning the alder-tree had grown
another foot; and Thule and his mother
watched the growing leaves, and touched
them with reverent fingers. They were certainly of a tender green, lined with shining
silver.

"May Odin favor my pretty alder!" said
Thule; "nor let the frost pinch it, nor the
winds blacken its green buds!"

Then Thule kissed his mother, and trudged
off to the forest as usual. But he seemed
doomed to adventures; for this time he was
met by three armed men, who were roaming
the country as if seeking something.

"Prithee, little urchin," said one of the
men, "can you tell us what has become of a
young alder-tree, whose green leaves are
lined with silver?"

"I dug up an alder-bush, kind sirs," replied the boy, trembling, and remembering that his mother had said she was almost afraid of that little tree.

"There are many alder-bushes," said another of the men gruffly; "but only one is green at this time of year, and has silver-lined leaves. It was placed here by command of the giant Loki, and no one was to touch it under pain of death; for, when his mountain-garden should be laid out in the spring, the tree was to be uprooted, and planted therein."

Thule grew almost as stiff and white as if a frost-giant had suddenly breathed on him. He knew that Loki was a pitiless god, feared by all, and beloved by none,— a god who had an especial grudge against the whole human race.

"I will hold my peace," thought Thule.

"I will never confess that the tree I carried away has silver-lined leaves. I will hasten home, pluck up the bush, and burn it: then who will be the wiser?"

But Thule, in spite of his trembling, could not forget his good mother's counsel: —

"Your words, my boy, let them be truth, and nothing but truth, though a sword should be swinging over your head."

Then, as soon as his voice returned to him, he confessed that the tree he had removed was really just such an one as the men described, and begged for mercy, because, as he said, he had committed the sin ignorantly, not knowing the mandate of the terrible giant.

But the men bade Thule lead them to his mother's house, and point out his stolen treasure; declaring that they could show no mercy; for, when Loki had made a decree, no man should alter it by one jot or one tittle.

"Oh!" thought the unfortunate boy, wringing his hands, and trembling till the woollen tassel on his cap danced a gallopade, "oh, if the cruel night-elf, who led me into this mischief, would only come forward now, and help me out of it! But, alas, it is of no avail to invoke him; for it is now broad daylight, and the sun would strike him into a stone image in a twinkling."

When Thule, followed by the messengers of Loki, had reached the door of his cottage, he found his gray-haired mother sprinkling the roots of the beautiful alder, and fondling its leaves with innocent pleasure. At sight of the armed men, she started back in affright.

"It is indeed the giant's tree," said the men to Thule. "Pluck it up, and follow us with it to Loki's castle on the mountain."

"To Loki's castle!" shrieked the wretched

mother. "Then he must pass a frightful wilderness, be assailed by the frost-giants; and, if there be any breath left in him, Loki will dash it out at a glance! Have mercy on a poor old mother, O good soldiers!"

The unhappy boy touched the tree, and it came out of the ground of its own free will; and, in a trice, stood on its feet, shook out its branches into arms, and in another moment was no longer a tree, but a child, with a beauty as dazzling as sunshine.

"Unfortunate men!" said she, in a voice whose angriest tones were sweeter than the music of an Æolian harp, "unfortunate are you in being the servants of Loki! Go, tell your cruel master that the schemes he has plotted against me and mine have all failed: my enchantment is over forever. Yonder boy," said she, pointing to little Thule, "has saved me. I was, and still remain, an elf of light, as playful and harmless as sunshine. The merciless Loki, enraged at the love I bear the children of men, changed me to a little alder-tree, which is the emblem of girlhood. But he had no power to keep me in that form forever. He was obliged to make a condition, and he made the hardest one that his artful mind could invent: 'Since you love mortals so dearly,' said he, 'no one but a mortal shall free you from your imprisonment. You shall remain a tree till a good child shall touch you,—a child who is generous enough to SHARE HIS LAST LOAF WITH A STRANGER, honest enough to GIVE BACK A REWARD FOR HIS HONESTY, brave enough to SPEAK THE TRUTH WHEN A LIE WOULD HAVE SAVED HIS LIFE. Long shall you wait for such a deliverer!'

"Now how amazed will Loki be when he learns that this little boy has been tempted in all these particulars, yet proves true. My poor soldiers, you may return whence you came, for the alder-tree will never rustle its silver leaves in the mountain-garden of Loki."

Then the men disappeared, not sorry that the good boy had escaped his threatened doom.

Thule, looking at the beautiful elf so lately a tree, could hardly trust his own eyes; and I fancy that many a boy, even at the present day, would have felt rather bewildered under the circumstances.

"Shining.child!" said he: "you look vastly like the wonderful little being who led me out of the forest yesterday."

"That may well be," replied the elf of light; "for she is my sister. The brown dwarf who pointed out to you the alder-tree is also an excellent friend of mine, though, strange to say, I have never seen him. We love to aid each other in all possible ways; yet we can never meet, for there is a fatality in my eyes which would strike him dead. He had heard of Thule, the little woodcutter who was called so brave and generous and true. He tried you, you see; and so did my frolicsome sister, who was fairly ablaze with delight when she found you could not be tempted to steal!"

Thule's mother had stood all the while on the threshold, overawed and dumb. Now she came forward, and said, —

"I am prouder to-day than I should be if my son had slain ten men on the battle-field!"

The beautiful elf of light, penetrated with gratitude and admiration, remained Thule's fast friend as long as he lived. She gave the lad and his mother an excellent home, and made them happy all the days of their lives.

THE PRINCESS HILDA.

PRINCESS HILDEGARDE sat at an open window, looking out upon her garden of flowers. She was very beautiful, with a face as fair and sweet as a rose. Not far off sat, watching her, her young cousin Zora, with a frown on her brow.

There was bitter hatred in Zora's heart because Hildegarde was rich and she was poor; because Hildegarde would, in time, be a queen, and she one of her subjects. Moreover, Hildegarde was so beautiful and good that the fame of her loveliness had spread far and wide; and it was for her beauty that Zora hated her more than for any thing else.

In childhood Zora had been very fair; and the courtiers had petted her, and pronounced her even fairer than the princess; but her beauty had never meant any thing but bright eyes and cherry cheeks: so it could not last. If she had only cherished pure thoughts and kind wishes, she might still have been as lovely as Hilda; but who does not know that evil feelings write themselves on the face?

Jealousy had pulled her mouth down at the corners; deceit had given it a foolish smirk; spite had plowed an ugly frown in her brow; while she had tried so many arts to make her rich brown skin as delicately white as Hilda's, that it was changed to the tint of chrome yellow.

It was said in those days, that Zora was in the power of wicked fairies, who twisted her features into the shape that pleased them best.

At any rate, how the amiable Princess Hilda was to blame for all these deformities it would be hard to say; and she little dreamed of the malice in her cousin's heart.

But, while Hilda was looking out of the window, a noble knight passed that way; and so delighted was he with the rare sweetness of her face, that he forgot himself, and paused a moment to gaze at her. The princess blushed, and let fall the silken curtain; but Zora had seen the knight, and knew he was the royal Prince Reginald. She ground her teeth in rage; for she had determined that the prince should never see her beautiful cousin.

"They shall not meet," said she to herself: "no, not if there are bad fairies enough to prevent it."

But, when the princess looked up, Zora was smiling very sweetly. Who could have dreamed that she was thinking of nothing but how to ruin the peace of her gentle cousin?

Zora could hardly wait for nightfall, so eager was she to do her wicked work. When it was dark, and all was quiet, she stole out of the castle, wearing a black mantle which hid her face.

"Now," thought she, "no one can recognize me, and I will seek the fairy Gerula."

You must know that Gerula was one of the most wicked and hideous sprites that ever existed. She dwelt in a cave far from the abodes of men. It was hidden by huge trees, through which the wind never ceased howling. At evening owls hooted overhead, and many creeping things wound their length along the ground. The more toads and snakes she could see about her, the better was she pleased; for fairies, as well as mortals, are attracted by what is akin to themselves.

She was descended from a race called kobolds or goblins; and she loved all the metals which lie under the earth as well as the living things which crawl up out of its bosom.

So acute were her ears, that she heard Zora's steps from a great distance. She brushed back her elf-locks, and gave a low grunt like some wild beast. It pleased her that the Lady Zora should find need of her counsel; but, when Zora had reached the cave, the cunning fairy pretended to be sleeping, and started up in seeming surprise.

" What brings a body here at this time of night?" said she.

"I am Lady Zora. I have come, sweet fairy, to beg a favor. The Princess Hilda is hateful to me: work one of your charms on her, and let me see her face no more."

The old fairy pricked up her ears and said to herself, "Ha! ha! I will have nice sport out o' this!" then said aloud, "Say, what harm has the princess done to my rosebud, my lily, my pride?"

Zora's eyes flashed. "Prince Reginald has seen her; and to see her is to love her. My heart is set on wedding Prince Reginald. Take her out of his way!"

Just then a broad gleam of moonlight fell on the treacherous maiden. It was strange how much she looked like the cruel fairy; and Gerula gazed on her with delight.

"My beautiful viper!" said she, using the sweetest pet-name she could think of, "I will do your bidding. But first say what you will give me if I put Hildegarde out of your way."

Then she chuckled, and rubbed her hands in great glee. Zora started back in alarm.

"I did not know you sold your charms for gold; but I would give you half my fortune if need be, any thing, to be rid of Hilda."

The fairy chuckled again. "Just the damsel for me," thought she.

"I will give you a diamond necklace," said Zora: "it is worth a small kingdom, and was given me by my cousin Hilda. You can surely ask no more?"

"Diamonds!" said the goblin, snapping her fingers. "What think you I care for them? Do I not tire of stooping to pick them up? for they are given me by my cousins, the gnomes, any day. No diamonds for me! Keep them and your gold. I ask but one thing, my dear."

Here she spoke in low hissing tones, more terrible than her loudest croakings.

"Promise me, if you do not marry Prince

Reginald, you will let me change you into a charming green snake."

" Alas !" cried Zora, turning pale, "who ever heard of such a cruel request ? "

" Cruel, am I ? " said the goblin in delight. " Oh, I must seem cruel to one who is so gentle and lovely as Hilda ! "

" Alas," cried Zora, " I may fail to win Prince Reginald."

" All the better," chuckled the fairy. " When you become a snake, you and I shall enjoy each other's society, I assure you."

Zora shuddered.

" But it's all one to me," added the goblin, beginning to yawn. " On the whole, I think you may as well go home."

Zora wrung her hands, and groaned.

" Yes," said the gnome : " go back to the castle. Ugh! I would sooner trust one of my winking owls to do a daring deed than you! Fie upon you! Creep back to your bed, and let Hilda marry the prince: a lovely pair they will make. Off with you, for I have to make up my sleep I have lost."

But Zora was thinking.

"I am silly indeed!" she said to herself. "Why do I fear that I shall not win the love of Prince Reginald? Only Hilda stands in my way." Then she said aloud, —

"Lovely being! sweetest of all the race! Great as is my horror, I will consent to your will."

Just then was heard a crackling in the dry leaves.

"Only a snake," said the goblin. Zora trembled.

"Will you promise me that Hilda will never trouble me again?"

"I promise," said the goblin, with one of

her merriest laughs, as loud and hoarse as the song of a frog.

Just then a sigh was heard not far from the place where Zora stood. "There is some one here : we are watched," she whispered. But Gerula thought it the howling of the wind ; for she was busily musing over the charm she was about to obtain of her cousins, the gnomes, and her eyes and ears were not as sharp as usual.

She took from the ground her crooked staff.

"Hush," said she ; "if the sky were to fall on your head, you are not to speak ; for now begins the charm."

Then she drew a circle three times on the ground, with her staff, and said in low tones, —

"Hither, ye cousins, that come at my call :
    The princess is young and fair ;
  Mix me a charm that shall bring her to woe
    Spin me your vilest snare."

A mist arose, in which Zora could see dim figures, one after another. Zora held her breath. Gerula muttered again in low tones, —

> " Hilda is gentle, and dreams of no guile ;
>   The little gnomes sit and weep ;
> ' Make her, — if *must* be, — a snowy wee lamb,
>   In the fold with her father's sheep.' "

Zora clapped her hands in delight. But just then, a faint sound was heard, as of some one talking between the teeth. Then Zora spoke, and the charm was broken. She did not intend to speak; but asked, " What noise was that ? " before she thought.

" You have broken the charm," said the fairy. "The soft-hearted gnomes are unwilling to punish Hilda ; but I hoped, by my craft, I could force them to keep her a lamb forever; or, at most, to let her grow to a sheep, and die by the knife.

"I will now weave a new charm; but I fear me they will repent; and Hilda will not be got out of the way, after all. Not a word more, I warn you."

So saying, the goblin made another circle three times on the ground, and again muttered, —

" How long is fair Hilda a snowy wee lamb?
  The little gnomes cry, ' We fear
Till comes a brave lion so tender and true,
  She lives by his side a year.' "

Zora clapped her hands again. "That is well," said she, "for never was a lion seen who could let a little helpless lamb pass his way without tearing it in pieces."

"True," said the gnome, well pleased, "it has worked well. Hilda will never trouble you again: so creep home softly, and go to your rest: dream of bats and creeping snakes; and to-morrow, at sunrise, ask your cousin to walk with you in the park. Now adieu!"

"Adieu, sweetest and best of fairies!" said Zora, drawing her silken mantle closely about her face. As she left the hideous cave, snakes hissed after her, and a bat flew in her face; but she had sold herself to evil, and walked on without fear of the creatures she so strongly resembled.

Next morning, at the first peep of the sun, she cried, "Awake, dearest Hilda, joy of my life, and walk with me in the park. I have lost my diamond necklace; and last night I dreamed it was lying in the grass."

So Princess Hildegarde opened her eyes, and hastened to follow her cousin; for her heart was quickly moved to any act of kindness.

"What a fine flock of sheep!" cried Hilda,

as they were walking in the park. "Such innocent" ——

She would have said more, but the words on her tongue were suddenly changed to tender bleatings; and even as Zora stood looking at her, she crouched down on all fours, dwindled in size, was enveloped in white fleece, and became a dumb lamb.

Overwhelmed with horror and surprise, she raised her pleading, tearful eyes to the face of her cousin. But Zora gave a mocking laugh, and said, pointing her finger at her, —

"Who now is the heir of the throne? Will they set the royal crown on a sheep's head, think you? Bravo, sweet creature! You may stand now between me and Prince Reginald as much as you please. It's all my work. I tell you once for all, I hate you, Hildegarde."

Was this Zora's return for her cousin's love? The princess would fain have expressed her grief and amazement.

"Pray don't try to talk, my bonny wee thing! It is not one of your gifts, at present. Your voice has ceased to be musical. I can sing now as well as you. Go to nibbling grass, deary, and a long life to you!"

Then the treacherous Zora turned on her heel, and left her poor cousin to her mute despair.

A search was made far and wide for the missing princess. Forests were hunted, rivers were dragged; but without avail. Deep gloom fell on the people, and the queen nearly died of sorrow. They all believed Hilda dead, all but Zora, who knew too well her cruel fate.

Then Zora was treated like the king's daughter. Wherever she went, there were servants to follow her; yet none loved her, and behind her back they made wry faces, and said she looked like one who was tormented by evil fairies.

But, alas for Zora, nothing more was seen of Prince Reginald. She watched the windows day after day, hoping to see him ride by on his coal-black steed; but he never came. Then she grew crosser than ever, and the frown on her brow ploughed deeper still. She dreamed every night of horrible goblins and slender green snakes.

All the while, poor Hildegarde roamed about the park. The other lambs were content to nip the sweet grass, and frisk in the sun; but the princess remembered something better, for her soul did not sleep.

The king himself, in his walks, was struck with the beauty of the lamb; its fleece was far softer, finer, and whiter than was common.

He said to his chief shepherd, "Watch well yonder snow-white lamb, and give it particular care."

For there was something in its soft dark eyes, as they were raised to his face, which stirred the king's heart, though he knew not why.

One day the city was thrown into a great tumult. A lion had been seen in the thicket which bordered the park. The huntsmen, hearing of it, stole out privately to waylay him in a snare. He was caught alive by the king's favorite huntsman. It was agreed that such a fine lion had never been seen before ; and the king ordered a strong iron cage for the beast, and made his favorite huntsman his keeper.

. Now the cage was in the midst of the park; and such was the terror of the sheep and deer, that none of them went near it.

"I will go," thought poor Hildegarde; "let the lion tear me in pieces. Sooner would I perish, than live on, a poor wee lamb all my days."

So she went up to the cage, though with a faint heart; but the lion put his paw out of the bars, and stroked her face, as if he would bid her welcome. The keeper reported the fact with great surprise.

It may be that the beautiful brown eyes of the lamb tamed the fierce spirit of the lion; for they were human eyes, full of Hildegarde's own soul. Be that as it may, the lamb went every day to the cage, till the lion learned to watch for her, and gave a low growl of joy when he saw her coming. At last the keeper ventured to drop her carefully into the cage. The lion was beside himself with joy; and, after that, the lamb was placed in the cage every morning, and only taken out at night.

Then the king invited all the noblemen into his park, to see the strange sight of a lion and a lamb living together in peace. And all the while Hildegarde loved her shaggy companion, and asked herself every day how it could be that a lion should have such speaking eyes and such a tender heart. But she almost believed that he was a human being, shut up, like herself, in a cruel disguise.

At last, when a whole year had gone by, the time came for Hilda to be disenchanted; for the good little gnomes had declared that if she could live for a twelvemonth in peace with a lion, the charm would then be at an end.

Hilda did not know this; but awoke at sunrise, and, going to drink, saw the image of her old self in the fountain; and faint voices repeated in chorus these lines: —

"Thrice welcome, sweet Hilda! the little gnomes say
    At sunrise their charms shall end;
  So go to the lion, and open the cage;
    The prince is your own true friend."

This was so sudden and unexpected that the happy Hilda could hardly believe her senses. She gazed at her jewelled fingers; she touched her velvet robe. "It is Hildegarde," said she dreamily; "where has she stayed so long?"

She went to the cage; and, finding the key hanging on the outside, would fain have freed the poor lion, but thought of the terror it would cause the sheep and deer, and dared not do it.

She put her soft white arms within the bars, saying, —

"You have been a true friend to the little white lamb. She has found her tongue again, and can say so. Kind old lion, gentle prisoner, Hildegarde will not forget you."

The noble beast looked at the disenchanted princess, and the next instant was changed to his true form; and, in place of a tawny lion, it was the brave Prince Reginald. Hilda blushed with joyful surprise, and would have taken down the key to unlock the cage, but the prince said, —

"Loveliest Hildegarde, will you be my bride? Speak before you unlock the cage; for, if you say nay, Reginald must again become a dumb beast, and, as he has been for a year, so will he be for the rest of his days."

Hildegarde cast down her eyes, and answered, "If so be the lion and the lamb could live side by side for a year, may not Reginald and Hilda dwell together in peace?"

"Then," said the joyful Prince Reginald, "I pray thee unlock the cage."

Now, as they walked together in the park.

the prince told Hildegarde, that he had loved her for a twelvemonth and a day.

He described Hilda's visit to the cruel goblin. He said that he himself had overheard the two talking together, had ground his teeth, and sighed. Then the gnomes, seeing his grief, had come asking him if he would be changed for a year, and maybe for life, into a lion; and for Hildegarde's sake he had gladly consented.

Hearing all these things, the grateful princess wept, and said, —

" Now I know that Prince Reginald is my own true friend."

The prince led Hilda to the palace, and presented her to the king and queen. Great was the wonder, and loud the rejoicing throughout the land.

The treacherous Zora was seen no more, but was changed into a slender green snake;

and the king said she deserved her fate ; "for, mark you," cried he, "there is no crime worse than to play false to those whom we pretend to love."

But Prince Reginald and Hildegarde were married, and lived in peace all the rest of their lives.

GOLDILOCKS.

" A king lived long ago,
In the morning of the world,"

who had two children, Despard and Goldilocks. They were twin brother and sister,
but no more alike than a queen-lily and a
nightshade, a raven and a dove.

Goldilocks was a bright young damsel,
with hair like fine threads of gold, and a face
so radiant that people questioned if the blood
in her veins might not be liquid sunshine.
Her eyes were as soft as violets; and her
laugh was like the music of a spring robin.

Despard, on the other hand, was as melan-
choly as an owl. His raven hair cast gloomy

shadows, and his mournful eyes pierced you with a sudden sorrow. He was too low-spirited to chase butterflies, weave daisy-chains, and dance with Goldilocks among the flowers. He liked better to play at a mimic funeral, and deck himself as chief mourner, in a friar's robe with sable plumes. He could never understand why laughing Goldi-locks should object to making believe die, and be buried in the large jewel-coffer, which stood for a tomb.

He always said that, if he lived to be a man, he should grow all the more wretched, and creep over the earth like a great black cloud. When Despard spoke so hopelessly, Goldilocks paused in her song or her play, and stealthily brushed a rare tear from her eye. She was afraid her brother's words might prove true.

These children lived in what is called the

Golden Age, when the rivers flowed with milk and wine, and yellow honey dripped from oak-trees. Their childhood would probably have lasted forever; but the Silver Age came on, and every thing was changed. Then, it was sometimes too warm, and sometimes too cold. People began to live in caves, and weave houses of twigs. The king, their father, died, and went, so it was said, to the " Isles of the Blessed."

The children were shipwrecked upon a foreign shore, all because of a sudden swell of the ocean. Here they were desolate and homesick. The strange people among whom they had fallen did not know they were the children of a king. No one was left to care for them but their old nurse, named Sibyl.

This aged woman was growing lame, and her hair was gray; yet she loved the twins, and would spin all the day long, to buy black bread for them, and now and then a little choice fruit.

"Alas," she sighed, "alas, for the Golden Age, when the forests had never been robbed, when oxen were not called to draw the plough, and the beautiful earth laughed, and tossed up fruit and flowers without waiting to be asked!"

The frocks that Sibyl made for Goldilocks were coarse; but on fair spring days she took from the chest a delicate, rosy robe, embroidered with gold, and smiled to see how it adorned the child.

But as for Despard, she had no hope that he would ever look well in any thing. She would part Goldilocks' wonderful hair, and say,—

"Old Sibyl knows who is her love; she knows who would be glad to give her pomegranates and grapes, when she is too old to spin, and too weak to sit up."

Little Goldilocks would laughingly reply, —

" And I know, too: when I am a woman I
shall weave a net of my hafr, and fish up all
the gold that has sunk to the beds of the rivers. Then I know who will have a set of
hard gold teeth, and a silver rocking-chair."

" Thou art lovely enough to be a goddess,
little Goldilocks. And what wilt thou do
with the rest of the gold ? "

" Oh, Despard shall have all he can carry;
for Despard is good, let people say what they
may. And I will have a crown made for him,
with diamonds set in it as plenty as plums in
a pudding."

" Listen, my children," said the old Sibyl,
sadly : " there will be no one to give me
grapes and pomegranates when I am faint
and weak. I can read by the stars that you
are soon to go on a pilgrimage, and leave

your old nurse behind. You may well weep, my good little boy: there is to be no rest for your feet till you have travelled over the whole world, from north to south."

Despard groaned aloud; but Goldilocks clapped her hands and laughed. "Oh, let us start to-night," she cried.

"When the sun-god has made twelve journeys in his winged boat," sighed Sibyl, "and when the young moon has arisen out of the ocean, then you may go."

And, at the appointed time, the faithful nurse, with many tears, prepared her foster-children for their long journey. She took from a worm-eaten coffer some family heir-looms, which had been lying since the days of the Golden Age, enveloped in rose-leaves and gold paper.

She placed in the hand of Despard a dagger with a jewelled hilt, a quiver of poisoned

arrows, and a glittering sword, with a blade
sharper than a serpent's tooth.

But to Goldilocks she gave a flask of
smooth, fragrant oil, a vase of crystal-bright
water, and a fan made of the feathers of the
beautiful bird of Paradise.

Kissing the little pilgrims, she said, —

"These gifts have been saved for you
these many years : use them as an inward
voice shall whisper you: I give you my blessing.   The gods attend you!   Farewell."

The children at first walked on sorrowfully; but soon the gay spirits of Goldilocks
rebounded, and she waltzed hither and thither, like a morsel of thistle-down.

"See, brother," said she, "we almost fly !
What a glorious thing it is to go on a pilgrimage !   I am glad the beautiful Silver
Age has come, and Jupiter has given us
leave to take a peep at the world !"

"All very well for you to say," moaned Despard; "you flit about as if you had wings on your feet; while, as for me, it is true I move with equal speed, but so painfully that I wonder my footprints are not stained with blood."

Soon the children observed, not far off, a party of youths rowing on the bosom of a lake. They sat in a rocking, unsteady little bark, but were in gay spirits, blowing bubbles, watching idle clouds, and throwing up empty shouts to be caught up and echoed by the hills.

"I wish we had not seen these happy people," sighed Despard; "for, if you can believe me, sister, I really feel as if I must pelt them with my arrows."

So saying, little Despard began to fire his poisonous darts at random.

"Why, brother," cried Goldilocks, in alarm,

"are you possessed by the furies? Take care how you aim, or you will surely do mischief."

Even as she spoke, several of the gay youths dropped to the bottom of the boat, apparently wounded. Their companions pushed for the shore; and Goldilocks almost flew, to pour into the red wounds her brother had made the smooth healing oil from her flask.

"Poor dears," said she, pitying their pain, "I have done my best; and, see! these ugly gashes are almost healed. I cannot promise you, though, that they will not leave scars."

The youths thanked the sweet girl, and assured her it was almost a pleasure to be wounded, if one might be nursed by such gentle hands as hers. But as for Despard, it was hardly strange that they should look upon the poor boy as a wicked little highwayman; or, at best, a saucy, careless fellow.

Some of the older youths, however, patted him on the shoulder, and said, "For your sweet sister's sake we can even endure your pranks."

"Do not despise me," said the boy, sadly; "for as I am moved, so must I do. Not for the whole world would I fire a poisonous arrow, if the mighty Jove did not compel me."

As they walked on, Despard, against his will, flung into the air a quantity of winged torments, which he found stowed away in his wallet, such as gnats, wasps, and flies.

"There, now," said sweet Goldilocks, ready to weep, "why could you not look before you, and see those pretty children playing yonder in that fragrant meadow?"

"I saw them," said Despard; "but what good did that do?"

"O brother, I wish the Golden Age would

come again, and then you would cease scattering mischief and trouble."

The little ones, suddenly stopped in their play by the army of insects, ran hither and thither over the meadow, screaming with pain. But Goldilocks appeared in the midst of them, with her shining hair, violet eyes, and laugh like the music of a spring robin.

"Come to me," said she ; "let me kiss away the stings."

In a very short space the children were soothed, and had forgotten their trouble. Then they threw their little arms about Goldilocks' neck, and begged her to stay and play with them.

"Sweet children, it is my mission, — so the stars say, — to travel all over this world, from north to south. But, for all that, I will frolic with you till the sun sets."

"Will the sad boy come too ? " asked the children.

Goldilocks shook her bright curls. "He is planting a garden," said she; "no need to ask him; he hears nothing while he is at play, and his games are as solemn as midnight."

The children made believe that the beautiful Goldilocks, in her rose-colored dress, with her beaming hair and flying feet, was a great butterfly, which they were trying to catch. Now here, now there, the glowing butterfly flitted from flower to flower, leading her followers a merry chase. Every child thought to seize and hold her, for a kiss. She laughed; and the breezes danced with her hair, like —

> " Zephyr with Aurora playing,
>   As he met her once a-Maying."

But before any one had kissed or even touched her, she had disappeared, leaving the children gazing into the air, and seeking their late companion with tearful eyes.

Goldilocks had only gone back to Despard, who was still planting flower-seeds.

"What a miserable game," said Goldilocks ; "it is worse than playing funeral ! Who thought you could make flowers grow ? Our old nurse said it was only Demeter, the goddess, who could do that.   Here, now, you have called up a bristling crop of thistles and brambles ! On my word, Despard, it is a pity !"

" Well, well, Goldilocks, see what you can make of them.   I am doomed to work, though I don't wish it ; and my work is always disagreeable, though I can't tell why !"

Goldilocks knelt, and blew on the prickly plants with her sweet breath. By the nodding of the next breeze, they were changed to roses, violets, and hare-bells.

"It is pleasant to see any thing smile, even a flower," said Goldilocks, laughing as she spoke.

"I think," replied Despard, " that this is a strange pilgrimage. I believe our very thoughts are alive. I wish I could stop thinking."

By and by they came to a rude house, — as fine a one, though, as people in the Silver Age had yet learned how to build. Despard paused, and knocked gently. "Why linger here?" whispered his sister.

" I know not," sighed the boy, " but so must I do."

"How now, little ones? you startled me so!" cried a woman, opening the door by the width of a crack.

"Let us come in," said Despard, sorrowfully; " we are two little wanderers; and our hairs are wet with night-dews."

"Come in, then, little ones, and welcome; but never, at any one's door, knock so loud again," added the woman, pressing her hand against her heart.

"I only tapped with the ends of my fingers," said the boy.

"Ah," said the woman, "it was louder to me than thunder." Then, after she had set before them a supper of bread and milk, she rocked her baby, and sang to it a sweet cradle-song about mother Juno and high Olympus.

The children lay down on beds of rushes; and Goldilocks, soothed by the lullaby, fell asleep; but soon awoke, and saw her brother leaning, on tiptoe, over the osier basket. The baby's face looked, in the moonlight, white and pinched; and its sick hands were pressed together like two withered rose-leaves.

"Let me kiss him," whispered Goldilocks

smiling. But bitter tears rolled down Despard's cheeks. Drawing his little sword from its sheath, he pricked the baby's heart till one red drop, the life-drop, stained the steel. The sick baby ceased to breathe.

"O Despard, what have you done?" cried Goldilocks, seizing his arm.

"I know not," said the boy; "but as my heart moves me, so must I do."

Hearing voices, the mother awoke, and, as her habit was, turned at once to the cradle. The baby lay there beautiful and still; the pinched look gone, and its furrowed brow smoothed into a baby's smile. The mother wept bitterly.

"Ah, little stranger," said she, turning to Despard, "I knew you when I let you in. Why did I open the door for you?"

"Poor mother," said the boy sorrowfully, "if you had not opened the door, I must have come in by the window."

But Goldilocks threw her soft arms about the woman's neck, and comforted her till it was morning, and the " gilded car of day " had risen from the ocean. The tears on her cheeks she dried with her fan, made of magical feathers.

When the children set out again on their journey, the woman gave Goldilocks a loving kiss, and then embraced Despard, saying, —

" For the sake of your sweet sister, I love even you."

" Poor little brother," said Goldilocks when they had gone farther on their journey, " you are as good as I ; but how is it ? you make people weep, while I must go with you to dry the tears you call forth."

" I am a black cloud," groaned Despard, " you a sunbeam."

" But I like to have a cloud to shine on," said loving little Goldilocks.

Footsore and weary, the little pilgrims travelled on; and, when they had gone from north to south, and back again, the Sibyl met them with tender kisses; and, when they were refreshed, bade them go forth again.

"For," said she, "this world is always new, my dears. The people who are born to-day were not here yesterday; and every mortal must see the faces of my foster-children."

It was now the Brazen Age, and Despard and Goldilocks had grown to be a youth and maiden; but still they travelled on. The Iron Age came; and Despard's raven hair was frosted; but Goldilocks' curls never faded. Let her live as long as live she may, she can never grow old.

Their pilgrimage is not over yet; nor will it be while the earth revolves about the sun.

12

The brother and sister come to every house; they knock at every door.

To all the children who open their eyes upon the light, come Despard and Goldilocks, the bitter and the sweet of life, the twin angels of Happiness and Sorrow.

THE END.